footprints

footprints

by shelby hearon

alfred a. knopf   new york   1996

This Is a Borzoi Book
Published by Alfred A. Knopf, Inc.

Copyright © 1996 by Shelby Hearon

All rights reserved under International and Pan-American
Copyright Conventions. Published in the United States by
Alfred A. Knopf, Inc., New York, and simultaneously in Canada
by Random House of Canada Limited, Toronto. Distributed
by Random House, Inc., New York.

Portions of this book appeared in different form in
Southwest Review.

Library of Congress Cataloging-in-Publication Data
Hearon, Shelby.
Footprints / by Shelby Hearon.
p. cm.
ISBN 0-679-44641-9
1. Married women—United States—Fiction.
2. Adult children—Death—Fiction.
I. Title.
PS3558.E256F6 1996
813'.54—dc20 95-42853 CIP

Manufactured in the United States of America
First Edition

To the beloved friends who helped me on this book

Judith Jones
Kay and Eddie Mayer
William Halpern

EX LIBRIS

GIFT OF

SIMI VALLEY FRIENDS
OF THE LIBRARY

If I am not you, I cannot grasp what it is like to be you.
I can perhaps conjure up the missing shade of blue, but
I cannot conjure up the missing shade of you.

Consciousness Reconsidered
OWEN FLANAGAN

footprints

I

Someone in this crowd is wearing our daughter's heart. I imagined Douglas thinking those words. We were holding hands, wife and husband, here at this outdoor picnic arranged to honor donor and recipient families. Earlier, there had been a ballgame between the medical staff and the organ staff, with recipients part of each team to show that they were good as new. There'd been a fine Texas barbeque (the first we'd had in years), pork loin, chicken legs, lean beef, to show that recipients could eat with hearty appetites. Soon there would be awards, speeches, the lighting of the torch.

Our marriage was breaking to bits against the shoals of this group of coastal folks who meant nothing but kindness. How could a marriage be buffeted to bits as if against a coral reef even while we bent toward one another, clasping warm palms together (the heat also a stranger to us), weighted by the anchor of twenty-five years?

To say that there was a difference in our point of view was to say the obvious, to say nothing really. For me, it wasn't a matter of the death of our daughter Bethany, or the decision to give some of what could be salvaged from what remained of her when she was gone. That I would deal with as I was able. It was Douglas's joy, his hope, his belief that it was *his daughter's heart* which was beating in someone's chest. That she still *was*, that twenty-two-year-old girl, woman, our lovely strong-legged runner. Had it been someone else, someone not Douglas, the man I thought I knew through and through, skin to flesh to very bone, my Douglas, I could possibly have taken it as metaphor, as a way of seeing a baton being passed. The baton itself is not the runner, yet it is part of the race.

But Douglas had made his reputation writing about the "I," the mind, about what made someone that someone. A biologist when we met, then neurobiologist, now generally called a brain scientist, he'd written books—*Storing the Mind* (an enlargement of his dissertation, *Minding the Store*), *The Matter of Mind* (his popular success), *Mind Fields* (the latest)—which had tried to add up all the short-cuts and long-cuts of the brain's amazing circuitry to explain what scholars called consciousness and the rest of us called ourselves. And that Douglas, the agreed-upon scientist in our house with the piece of paper to prove it, my thoughtful, wise husband, walking about in his navy jacket, khaki trousers, tasselled loafers, that Douglas, who was tapping his chest with two fingers sending a signal: We gave a heart. Is it yours? That Douglas was a stranger.

I held on to him, in reflex, as if not to let him swim away into the clusters of nervous, near-delirious family units, those who had given and those who had taken away. Chests opened from throat to navel on both sides, body parts traded much the

way children in their treehouse press cut wrists together, mingling blood, swearing lifetime connection.

Don't find him or her, I begged in the silence of my own
mind. Don't. Fail to make contact. Let our recipient have
decided to go away, to go fishing on Padre Island, to go see
a film, now that she's able to be up and about, so many movies
missed, or to go bowling, now that he can lift his big black
ball again.

It wasn't even the grave-robbing aspect of it—these beaming people with parts harvested from previous owners, like
cars with new valves or transmissions, accelerating around the
course again, the whistle blown, the flag dropped, the race
still on—that got to me. After all, in school at our respective
Chicago universities we'd explored all aspects of the question:
If every part of the bicycle is replaced, is it the same bicycle?

Rather, it was that Douglas, my Douglas, had become
Dr. Frankenstein, condemning our daughter to roam the earth
indefinitely, sewn up in someone else's chest. It was the almost mystical atmosphere. The near-séance. We are in touch
with your daughter, Professor Mayhall, she is sending you a
message. . . .

I joined two of the doctors from the medical complex.
One, Angleton, had done Bethany's transplant; the other was
a more famous, older man, straight-backed and slim. They
were talking between themselves about the progress that had
been made. How in the early days, most patients died. Talking about how the body never got used to foreign tissue, it
only learned to tolerate it. Recalling for each other the story
about the man who was on suppressants for nine years and,
thinking he was just fine, went off them and died within the
week. About the goat with the sheep's heart who lived and
had baby goats and grew old and, taken off the drugs, died in

a matter of hours. "They never get used to it," Angleton said, looking out at the happy parts carriers, medicated against rejection.

"That's why we're working on a pump," he explained. "Inorganic material is tolerated."

"It's the way a closed safety pin," I said, joining in, recalling a moment of panic when our son Bert was small, "can stay indefinitely in the body."

Nodding, the older doctor added, "Or an artificial hip."

I had been the one who'd initially given the go-ahead. We'd been called about the wreck, the unthinkable news, at eleven in the morning, Texas time. Some drunk driver had run a red light, hitting Bethany, who was headed for the brush country ranch over Thanksgiving break to see Daddy Mayhall's widow. We'd got to the Houston hospital where they had her late that night, to be met with the question: Would we consider a gift of life?

Several gifts, actually, it turned out. The lungs were too crushed. But the heart appeared fine. The liver also. The kidneys. What about tissue? Corneas? Skin and bones? Burn patients needed skin. Crushed and tumored femurs needed replacing. The lame wanted to walk again. The blind to see. Nothing that was donated would interfere with an open-casket funeral, we were assured. Bones were replaced with prostheses as quickly as they were harvested; removing skin appeared as a mild sunburn. I had told them yes. Yes. What did it matter? Bethany was gone. I had made myself think of a stone for her, under that giant live oak where Daddy Mayhall's stone was, at the ranch, with its baking summer, wide vistas, slow-feeding cattle.

I was frantic to reach Bert, off diving in some underground cave in the spongy, porous, hollowed-out world of north Florida, to tell him about his sister.

But Douglas, head in hands, had cried out, "No, God, not her eyes, I refuse." And so I'd told them: Organs but no tissue. And signed the lengthy, grisly forms.

Douglas, wandering the crowd, suddenly bounded forward, like a puppy sniffing a trail. Someone had beckoned to him, an elderly-looking black man dressed in a black suit, white shirt, a bright red tie with a red heart smack in the middle of it. A red hanky waving from the chest pocket. I didn't follow but stood with the medical team, watching as my husband bent down—the man with the red handkerchief was small, frail—tears coursing down his face. My Douglas, weeping as he had not at news of the wreck.

I'd not expected the recipient to be a man, since we'd been told the donor's heart had to be larger, that some function was lost in the transfer no matter how quickly they worked. But then Bethany, tall like her father, muscled, athletic, had weighed a dozen pounds more than the slight old man.

Reluctantly, I told the doctors I'd see them later, and crossed the grassy space in response to Douglas's call. My hand in his, I stood at his side. "He's just my age," my husband said, entranced by the idea. "Can you believe that? We were born the same week, the same year."

What did that have to do with anything? I wondered. That some boy born fifty years ago in a nearby Texas town had grown up to be kept alive by the offspring of some other boy born some two hundred miles away. What was the point? Was it the chanciness of it all? Or that the randomness didn't seem so random if the men had birthdays a week apart?

I shut my eyes, with effort opened them. "Nan Mayhall," I said, extending my hand. No need to hold myself back from this gentleman, whose attitude was certainly to be expected.

"The Reverend Calvin C. Clayton," he responded, pumping my hand, his seeming not much more than loose bones in a sock.

Then there was a murmur through the crowd, signalling that it was the time of day to get settled, time for the ceremony, the highlight of the show. I tugged Douglas away. "Don't," I pleaded. "Don't do this."

"It's a miracle," he said, his face still damp. "Can't you see?" His eyes filled again, and he wrapped his arms around me. "He said—" He broke down, got himself under control. "He said, 'Tell me your girl didn't take her own life.' And I said, 'No, no, she would never have done that. She loved life.' And he told me, 'Thank the Lord for that, I couldn't have stood it.' Can you imagine him worrying about a thing like that?"

"Douglas." What could I say? He stood transfixed, his neck exposed. The life expectancy of the good preacher with the red heart-stitched necktie prolonged with his own blood.

The Reverend Clayton was speaking, "—certainly a miracle. She was, they told us right off, type O, which is the universal donor, and I was type AB, which is the universal recipient, so they didn't have to bother with a lot of other matches. I can tell you we'd just about given up hoping. I was slipping right off the bedrock of this earth—"

Douglas leaned over to the man, now sitting upright on a nearby bench. "—for us, too, knowing that part of our Bethany still lives and breathes. You understand?" His voice shook.

I sat down by the man's wife, who was stitching a pink rosebud on a piece of white linen on which there were two rosebuds already, the cloth held tightly in place by a double hoop. A womanly sort of occupation, which my mom would have given half of her life to see her only daughter perform. "Hello," I offered, not sure what to say.

"My feet have given out," she confided.

"My feet are okay." I pointed to my black loafers, then to

my black tapered pants and white shirt. "We're still in winter in upstate New York. This was as summery as I could find for a Texas spring. We've been gone so long— It's my talking that gave out."

"My husband has been marking the days for this event."

"Mine, too." I studied the rounded face, the dark eyes looking through trim spectacles, and wondered how she felt about all of this, this woman, beyond being grateful that her man was around to mark off his calendar. Women were closer to the ground, as they said, closer to the matter of fact.

"You did a good thing," the preacher's wife allowed, tying a knot.

"She was already gone," I said.

"I know, but everyone doesn't see that." She peered at her handiwork, getting hard to see in the dusk.

"Thank you."

The staff people gave awards to the transplant teams and participating hospitals. They talked about the shared experience. The joy of hearing hope when there seemed to be no hope; the joy of giving the gift of that hope. The solace of knowing that someone was getting a second chance because of your generosity. They talked about courage: the courage to give and the courage to receive. To take heart from heartless happenstance.

A young man with sandy hair and a squeaky-clean white dress shirt and fresh-pressed jeans got up to speak. He was identified as the representative of the donor families. He started with an account of his wife, a Sierra Club hiker like himself, and the numerous climbs they'd taken together. Then, lowering his voice to a husky tremor, he talked about her cerebral hemorrhage, so young, only thirty-three, and how he'd given permission, knowing she would want this, for them to harvest whatever they could. Then he motioned to an older man in the audience, a balding and rather stocky man wearing a bright yellow bow tie. "This story isn't just mine," the young man said.

The balding man was introduced as a recipient. He picked up the story. How he'd plumb run out of air, was gasping like a drowning man, and how this young man and his wife had stepped in and thrown him a lifeline.

The climber resumed the tale, "So the two of us hiked to the top of Mount Elbert, in the Rockies if you don't know where that is, on her birthday, the way we'd planned to do it together, take our fiftieth hike, that's the big one, on her birthday. And"—here he had to stop and clear his throat, swallow a few times—"I can't tell you what it meant to me that Chuck here was willing to do that, you know, able to, what it meant to me that my wife's lungs hiked to the top of Elbert with me." He choked a minute, then added, "We crested the top together."

The two men embraced, and then lit the torch and held it high.

Douglas sat rubbing his streaming eyes. The preacher wiped streaks from his cheeks, then slapped a hand on Douglas's back. Douglas fumbled in both pockets, found his handkerchief. He turned and met my eyes, then turned away.

Grief cut a canyon there was no crossing.

❦   ⑥   ❦

Shortly after daylight, we headed west on I-10 toward the ranch, Douglas carefully sticking to the speed limit, both hands clenching the wheel as we passed the farm-to-market road where Bethany's drunk driver had accelerated into oncoming traffic, while I concentrated on not spilling the too-hot cafe coffee on my legs. We did not even try to talk as the farmlands grew scrubby with cedar brakes.

I'd sat up late in my nightgown reading the packet of material about "gifts of life" while Douglas turned lobster red in the shower. I'd wished that our son Bert was there to talk to; the material was grim. In the way that fathers and sons divide up the territory, he was a physiologist, an underwater breathing expert, almost as if to say: You took the mind, Dad, I'll take the body. Bert had lost friends, older men, experienced divers. Things happened to the oxygen mix or the rebreather equipment or they hit some hairpin twist in an underground cave. He could talk about bubbles and things going wrong and not confuse the accident with the buddy it happened to.

The donor, the guidelines explained, first had to be declared officially brain-dead. That was the term they'd given us for Bethany in November. But then we'd been spared the diagnostic details: was there doll's eye movement, was there nystagmus when the ear was irrigated with cold water, was there a gag reflex following bronchial stimulation with a suction catheter? Such brutal procedures to inflict on a still-breathing body with a still-beating chest. You had to know the patient was gone. I stuffed the pamphlet into the trash. How could Douglas, who called himself a brain scientist, think of Bethany as still alive?

I'd wanted to watch the transplant, although, as the doctors had explained, no one could operate with kin as spectators. It was difficult to put into words, for those who didn't understand on a gut level, that I needed to look at it from the other side, to separate out the process from the weight of my own grief. Loss, like pain, makes you self-absorbed. I wanted to see it standing in different shoes, and was aware at the time that somewhere in the hospital someone else (the nice Mrs. Reverend Clayton) sat also waiting, coffee growing cold, clock hands making their quartz clicks at slow speed.

"What transplant?" Bert had asked later when I'd told him. "Didn't they take Sis's liver, too," he said, "and a kidney? Three transplants?" His point was well-taken, of course; his point of view true. At last evening's event Douglas had not tapped his abdomen looking for a recipient, first his right side, then his left. We were invested in our hearts.

I'd mentioned my wish again to Angleton at the party and he had said, "Hmmmm"—not a bad response from a doctor. I hadn't pressed. "Let me see," he'd said.

"That boy last night—" Douglas broke the silence—"the one who climbed the mountain, seemed like a nice kid."

Nice kid. A verdict any son would wait light-years to hear. "Yes."

"Seemed all grown up, young as he was, not much older than Bert. I guess he had cause to be—" Douglas cleared his throat.

"The hiker lost his wife—" I bit my lip. It was very hard not to rise to Bert's defense, knowing as I did that in his heart of hearts my husband wished that his son had been there at the barbeque and celebration, had lit a candle, had told a story, had been a part of the tearful scene.

The ranch spread south of the San Antonio highway, about an hour and a half outside Houston, and it was a relief at last to turn into Daddy Mayhall's long drive, bump along the dry gravel, and pull up under the shade of a bent live oak. It felt strange not to be greeted by the sound of barking, but there were no longer dogs, cats, or even saddle horses now that Daddy's Mayhall's wife ran the place alone. She, Jesse, made a frequent complaining joke: If I was a man, folks would quit asking what I'm doing out here, on the south edge of nothing, me and the mesquite and the squatty palmettos and grasshopper frogs.

"You children look depleted," she said now, a big woman, with a good person's enveloping embrace. No longer red, her thick gray hair held high in a knot was laced with strands of faded rust, and she had a redhead's skin. "You ready for breakfast?"

"We are," I told her. "We waited to eat."

"Good thing." Jesse pulled Douglas to her, nearly his height. "Say, boy, where are your manners?"

He flushed a bit, then kissed her. "We've a lot to tell," he said.

"Tell it then over hash browns and deer-meat sausage."

While he complied, recounting the miracle of locating the recipient who had our girl's heart, using all the words of the night before (organ recovery, living will), I sank gratefully back into the sprawling house which had that thick-walled feel of places built long before central heat and air-conditioning, even though the white plaster was no longer limed, the exposed beams no longer supporting structure, the old open fireplace and hearth once used to cook now only used to warm the rooms in winter when a sudden norther hit.

From that afternoon, twenty-six years ago, when Douglas first brought me here, I'd burrowed into his boyhood home like a hermit crab slipping into a moon shell or a whelk. Fastening my rasps with such a grip that only a lit fire could have dislodged me, claiming it an ideal fit in an instant.

Douglas and I had met over apple strudel at a student hangout on the North Shore of Chicago. Hearing the familiar Texas accent at the next table, I had waved, and he had picked up his dessert plate and joined me. How amazing a coincidence it had seemed; we'd rocked back in our chairs in delight, hooked a finger in the belt of our jeans. From the hill country? From the brush country? Studying at Northwestern? At Chicago? Graduate work in paleontology? In biology? What needles in a Midwest haystack. What destiny.

I'd been defensive from the start. His background assumed scholarship; mine assumed school. That was my joke, my way of saying that I'd started out a dollar short and miles behind. My way of kidding around about the feeling that he'd been competing in the Olympics while I'd been running three-legged sack races. Public school education, I'd said, dealt in facts (the Battle of Goliad), private school education in theory (the bias of the observer in history). In private school, I'd said, my collecting trilobites, the physical specimens, would have seemed mundane, a tally; I would have been urged to debate the theories about natural selection, using them as examples. And, conversely, I said, Douglas would have been considered a flake in public school, pursuing the idea of consciousness, how we know that we know we know; he would have been seen as trying to bullshit his way out of the biology final. Douglas went along with me. "I forget you went to public school," he'd kid whenever I tried to make my point with concrete facts.

I hadn't been what Daddy Mayhall wanted when I showed up that first time on Douglas's arm. He'd wished his studious son to bring home some well-bred easterner whose (Boston or Westchester or Bucks County) folks owned a place on Nantucket. He was a mix of attitude, the old man—proud of the brains he'd raised, never failing to praise his boys, but feeling that their attributes were somehow something left over from a previous wife he'd never quite figured out, the mathematician who was in and out of his life like a parabola curve. He was conflicted about what he wanted for his boys, broad-shouldered Walter, built like his dad, and the younger boy, Douglas, who'd turned out downright handsome after having been a nerd as a kid. First off, he'd wanted them married well, to people of property, or at least of substance. If his sons wanted smart women, too, that was their privilege. Their right, you could say. Nothing wrong with that. Ranching women in Texas had always been smart as whips. They'd had to be—they usually ended up with the land, and with the money, too.

I'd come on like some foreman's kid. A tomboy in an age when cute as a button was the order of the day. Later, the style would be called unisex, and Daddy Mayhall would hate it still. Most of my free hours before I'd escaped to Northwestern had been spent hauling myself up the road to Burnet, Llano, Cherokee, San Saba, Mason. Digging in the stratified outcroppings, finding fossils. Trying to get a glimpse of some other time and place as far from my own as possible. Eons were barely far enough away to be safe. Light-years would have been better, but all I knew to study was what my hands could uncover. My love was trilobites, those three-segmented ancient animals layered in the Cambrian who'd stayed on this planet longer than anything else we knew. I'd been impressed by their incredible foresight. Possessing compound eyes, each with hundreds of lenses that corrected for astigmatism and night sight, they were able to see in all directions, unequalled vision for which they had no use at all on the muddy bottom of prehistoric seas. Why had they been so far ahead of themselves? Why had I?

But Daddy Mayhall was one to make the best of a situation. He perceived I was going to stick by his boy; plus he soon saw that I loved the ranch and could listen to his accounts of it until the cows came home.

Douglas had got to the end of his story, about the balding

man carrying the dead wife's lungs up Mount Elbert, about the lighting of the torch. I helped myself to another of Jesse's hot biscuits with honey. Grief made you ravenous. I had another deer-meat sausage.

Jesse refilled our cups. "You haven't hardly touched your hash browns," she said to her grown stepson, as if he was still in second grade. "Don't you know I am the only person alive who makes them as good as you can get at a truck stop?"

Douglas took a taste of the soft potatoes, crusted with paprika, cayenne, and grease. "They serve what they call home fries in the East," he said.

"I hear."

"Fries no home ever saw." He took a big bite while Jesse watched, but struggled to swallow it.

"That's like *homemade*," she chatted along. "That means they pour the mix in the sheet pan by hand. When you see that on the menu you know you can prepare yourself for a square: square biscuits, square muffins, square cake."

In the early years here, before our children came, Jesse had kept goats, dogs, cats, horses, a flux of domestic animals that she talked to incessantly. The big redheaded woman carrying on a conversation with Pettigrew, the orange tom, or Hildegarde, the German shepherd, while trooping across the backyard past Daddy Mayhall's current Lincoln Continental and his pickup trucks, to take the Appaloosas to pasture. ("Do you want to go or not, Hildy? You know you like nosing the ponies down to pasture, don't you?") It had made it possible for me, when I had babies, to talk up a storm to them, the same way Jesse had to her menagerie of animals.

I had to smile remembering the time, right after Douglas and I married, that I'd called her "Mother Mayhall," thinking that proper. She'd thrown herself on the floor on her back with her two arms and her two legs stuck up in the air like a dead horse. "That slays me," she said. "I'm flat on my back. Help me up, will you, come on, Nan, you put me down here. I didn't change *my* name when you got married, you changed *yours*, am I correct? And one of these days that business will grind to a halt, too. Then tombstones won't have to read: ELVIRA ARNOLD BLACKENSHIP TURNBALL WILLIAMS." She'd hooted and lifted her hair straight up as if it was on fire. "I kid you not," she'd declared. "The exact name of my grandmother's grandmother."

Now Jesse was retelling, settled back at the table, about the first time she met Douglas and his older brother. Her favorite, oldest tale.

"You remember hearing about this, Doug? I'd come to get to know you fellows, decide if I wanted to marry your daddy. We were still in the trial stage, you might say. I set right out and fixed you all hot chocolate with marshmallows and banana pancakes, a specialty of mine, as you'll recall. Walter was just eight, you were barely seven."

I liked hearing this story. It was the one Jesse always told, the way any family has its basic staples. How she was a young, spirited fiancée, coming out to the ranch house to spend the day with the kids who were about to become, by fiat, her stepsons. Her not having sense enough to be scared. And the first thing she sees is this eight-year-old boy, built stocky like his daddy, sitting at the kitchen table (the same one where we sat now) reading a book that looked to be a thousand pages long: H. G. Wells's *Outline of History*. "Where's your brother?" she asks, seeing one boy is missing, to which Walter replies, "He's doing a study of self-recognition." Oh, sure—here Jesse always rolled her eyes and tapped her head. At seven?

I remember thinking, when I first heard the story, that I'd

have known Douglas was a younger brother without being told. Younger brothers had narrower shoulders; no need for them to bear the weight of the world. Big brothers had already done that.

Jesse went on, "I ask him, 'Walter, can you read that?' I can't help myself, the words just come out. 'I think so,' he says, in that modest way smart kids have. And he does, to show me he is already into it: '—And first, before we begin the history of life, let us tell something of the stage onto which our drama is put—' "

Then she warmed to the part featuring Douglas, today's audience. How he comes through the kitchen door, carrying a full-length mirror, the skinny, framed kind that you tack up on the inside of closet doors, taller than him by a foot, just a thin sheet of black-backed glass. And how she and the older boy watch as he props the mirror up against a chair and makes clicking noises out the back door until a fat tabby tom comes in, stretches, sniffs at the bowl of Friskies, and catches sight of himself.

"And then, Doug," Jesse raised her voice and gestured to fill out her recital, "you move the mirror from side to side and that cat arches his back and shoots his tail in the air and hisses as big as you please. Then you move it again closer to him so he looks bigger and this time he reaches right around that frame, like he's after some cat on the other side of the mirror. Finally, he gives up, swats it, and races off to the back of the house.

"Next you get this little tablet down from your school shelf and write it all up with a pencil. Then you announce, 'I'm going to try a bird now.' I could have dropped my teeth, I tell you. Here is this little kid in corrective shoes and big spectacles, hauling this flimsy mirror out the door as big as you please. Like it was crackers and cheese.

"Your brother, Walt, who took it upon himself to educate me, explains it. Doug's interested, he says, in if we're the only animal who recognizes itself. The books say so, but he's got to find out for himself. He tried a cow, Dad let him go out to the pasture, but it didn't even know it was seeing anything. That makes the cat smarter. 'I bet pigs would know,' he says. 'Pigs are smarter than dogs or cats or horses.' And I tell him, 'I heard that, too.' And I'm glad I know something, at least.

" 'Even a baby knows,' Walt explains to me, like he is used to being the teacher. 'You can sit a baby in front of a mirror and it laughs and says its name. So it isn't something we learn when we get old enough to have ideas about self-reference, what I mean is,' he tells me in this serious way, 'it's innate.' And I say, 'I bet you're right.' And I'm thinking, Here is H. G. Wells in the kitchen, and outside in the yard not a tire swing or even a sandpile but your basic summertime fun self-perception experiment by the bird feeder."

Jesse looked fondly at her grown no-longer-bespectacled stepson. "I couldn't believe you wise old kids, your heads as full of ideas as the Scarecrow's was full of pins and needles. What had I got myself into?"

Douglas, who had heard this many times but always seemed to receive it as a blessing, said, "We were on our good behavior that day. We were showing off."

"Then your brother Walter says to me, 'I believe Mr. Wells is not thinking right. He says that the Chinese thought the world was flat and that the Greeks were the ones who figured out it was round. But you know he doesn't mean that all the millions of Chinese got together by the Wall and voted it was flat. Or all the Greeks got together in the Forum. I think it was one person who had the idea, and everybody listened to him.' And I could tell he meant to grow up and be that person." Jesse gestured to the living room, where the remaining picture of Walter lived.

"Then you come back in, Doug, this cocky, four-eyed kid, and say, 'I want to see what squirrels do,' and you show me where to find a sack of mixed nuts up behind the cornmeal and chili powder. Hazelnuts, hickory, black walnuts, pecans. A feast, I remember thinking, to make any bug-eyed squirrel give herself a second glance.

"And I wonder, where do children like you two send off your scholarly papers? You two amiable brains with appendages? And for a few minutes, I tell you, Doug, I think of just slipping out the door, leaving your daddy a note that says, 'Too late, honey, for me to make a dent.' But then I decide maybe you fellows can use a little help—"

Douglas looked embarrassed. At his past self maybe, or at his voluble stepmother's kindness. He nodded at her and I knew he was thinking that she'd told the story to take his mind off the previous evening. "I owe you one," he said, making a shaky smile, and then pushed away his plate.

I could always picture the young Douglas when I heard that story. Behind the tall, fair, attractive man he was, that small boy in spectacles holding that wobbly mirror half again his height, setting out to discover what in the world could see itself. Concluding that we are alone in that ability. Douglas, grown, still holding that mirror up, hoping to glimpse someone besides himself looking back.

Jesse was the best thing that ever happened to him. And to Walter, his brother, too, I guess, although I never got to know him. I used to look at the picture of him in the living room, taken in his pilot's uniform a couple of years before our wedding, standing in front of the wing of a bomber. His captain's cap on straight, his face, bearing a family resemblance, solemn. I used to wonder if he'd thought about the outline of history when he'd flown his missions.

♋ ⑥ ♋

Walking from the ranch house, we held hands the way we always had, walking through the morning haze that the sun hadn't baked off yet. The time of early morning when the cattle seemed beings from another planet, moving too slowly for ours, on another timetable, each bite chewed for as long as we take to eat a meal, each step taking the time it took us to cross a field. I'd often thought about that, about the *fed cattle*, as they called tomorrow's steaks, or, once, from Daddy Mayhall's point of view, tomorrow's stake in a few more head of beef. That they were aliens, surely. That if we'd encountered anything like that alighting from a spaceship (taking an hour to get down the ramp), we'd have made much of it. The same was true, of course, the other way, concerning those beings like hummingbirds who moved hundreds of times faster than we did. Each species had its own fingerprint of time.

I'd found a children's book for Bethany that I'd kept for Bert, since in that short time it had both gone out of print and out of the library. A little boy walks to school with a tortoise, an elephant, a horse, a dog, a butterfly. And by the end of his school day, it's the end of the butterfly's life. And by the end of his life, he's now got a white beard to his waist, the tortoise is coming home from his first day of school. That was the title, *First Day of School*. With all the fuss about censoring books, no one apparently remarked when death became banned.

"Jesse still takes the cattle to market," Douglas said. "She still studies the new breeds."

"Did you think she wouldn't?"

"I guess on some level. Dad always said he wanted somebody with enough sense to run the place after he was gone, and that was one reason he picked her, somebody younger and who had taken care of herself. Still, I suppose I'm like the people she complains about, wondering what she does out here all by herself all the time. I admit it. And that I wouldn't have wondered if he was here without a wife. I'd assume he needed running the place to keep his mind active. Not to get depressed—"

"Ranchers in Texas have always been mostly women."

"I know." Douglas tightened his grip on my hand. He was good about admitting what he saw as sexism. It didn't exactly change his view, but saying those things out loud got him to thinking. And he was just as quick to call me on it, whenever he heard something like, 'Men always . . .'

We got to the far fence and stood looking out at the vast grasslands that seemed to disappear in the mist, acres and acres, cattle dazed and grazing farther than the eye could see. Sleepwalking beasts, these creamy Charolais. Who would not have a clue a mirror was being held before their large oval eyes. Busy with bringing the cud up from their first stomach and chewing it at their leisure. Making that walk to school (the stockyards in their case) take a lifetime.

We stopped by the huge live oak at the back of the side pasture, a tree older than the ranch house, as old as the land, in a fertile field used now only in calving season. Three headstones stretched like a sleeper's arm from one side of the massive trunk. Jesse had bought and tended all three markers: Daddy Mayhall's, Walter's, and now, new and with that glossy look of unweathered granite, Bethany's. The old man's age more than theirs combined.

I touched my daughter's stone, circled the tree, then wandered off a bit to see how far I could see in all directions. I didn't know where Douglas's mind was, what this was for him, this pilgrimage. I knew that only one grave contained a casket, Daddy's; the others served only as memorials. Did that bother him?

I shaded my eyes to shut out the sight in the distance of my children, young, saddling up their horses, proud of being able to do so on their own, riding out for the afternoon, an empire of scrub-oak and cedar acres, and fences for the jumping. Bethany gripping tight with her jeaned knees, reins knotted and held in one hand; Bert hooking the stirrups with his boot heels, reins held separately, loose. Neither quite at home on animal-back. The girl preferring her feet on hard ground; the boy safer with water weighting him down.

"Bethany loved the ranch," Douglas said.

It bothered me the way people freely attributed feelings and opinions to those who had died ("He would have wanted us to . . ." "She would never have wished . . ."). The real person became invention; the real scraps of truth became buried in revision. "She came here when she could," I amended.

꿍   ⑥   꿍

Close to the old ranch house, we stopped. Both of us, perhaps, thinking at once of the big oak bed with its massive carved Mexican headboard where we'd always slept on our visits. A real lovemaking bed from which you could see for miles out the recessed windows, but which felt very private, being at the far end of the spread-out, thick-walled house.

How quickly we used to have sex. Back when we were courting and Daddy Mayhall was feeling responsible for keeping intact and out of trouble this smart-aleck girl that his

Dougie had brought home. There would be a sudden moment when the grown-ups had gone on ahead—to saddle up, or to pack a picnic in that year's Lincoln, and we would race together to our back room, Douglas and I. "Do we have time?" I'd whisper. "Sure," he'd say, reaching for me. "We got five minutes." And we'd shout with laughter, rip off our clothes, fling them everywhere, diving for the bed like it was a big swimming pool. Both so ready it was pathetic. And in those school days, both of us came almost at the first touch, anticipation having done its heady work.

Later, married, we still rushed back to the room after our early walk, or after Jesse's enormous breakfasts, to make love in the daylight, with the Mayhalls getting ready for the day, calling out to us.

As if remembering also, Douglas guided me along the wide outside stone walkway, getting to the familiar room without entering the main house. Once inside, in reflex, he threw the wood bolt on the door. After a minute, I pulled my red T-shirt over my head; I hadn't put on a bra. Douglas, watching me, his face unreadable, began to unbutton his plaid shirt. I went to him then and, on tiptoe, kissed his eyes, then his throat, then, lowering myself, the flat hard bone in the center of his chest, a private place. On the bed, he pushed my legs up, my knees against my breasts, and kissed my stomach before he got me wet. He'd used to do that, long kisses on my stomach, an incredibly erotic thing that we'd let go, forgotten. He used to do that and whisper, "Baby, baby, baby," not as endearment but as mantra. Wanting me to make a baby, another baby, lots of babies.

He'd get me aroused, and then he'd say it, "Baby, baby, baby," and sometimes I'd laugh and it would seem foolish and funny. But, increasingly, it grew to bother me. "Douglas," I told him, when we were not making love, "I don't want to have any more children. We have two. I think that it is an indulgence, a narcissism, to keep reproducing yourself. You have a houseful and it's for you; one or two always get the short end, feel neglected or cheated. Why do you press me to have more? Talk to me."

And Douglas would answer, "There were only the two of us, and then, after Walter died, well, I could see that if there'd been five of us it wouldn't have left such a gap. Or six. Or ten." Then he'd laugh. "A dozen?" But he had not really been thinking it through. Jesse—with stretch marks and back pain and fatigue and frustration at providing a backup crowd, a second string to come in if anything happened to the first team? That was obscene.

This had been a frequent fight, until we'd hit forty, until the children were in junior high. Now Douglas, kissing my stomach, whispered the words again, "Baby, baby, baby," and I wondered if he was back in the past or asking again. But I came and then he did and we stayed wrapped in each other's arms and legs until Jesse called out to us.

"Where have you lovebirds got to?"

∞　⑥　∞

We were preparing to leave, hoping to scoot between the worst shifts in Houston traffic, to catch the connecting flight to Syracuse. But it was hard to think about getting back in the car.

The sun had turned the view out the window yellow, mesquite-filtered yellow, and I watched Jesse, sun on her freckled arms, pack us up a travel feast, ham sandwiches and chocolate cake. I wondered if she had ever thought about another man, seriously. I knew the good-natured woman would never burden Douglas with the concept that she'd re-covered from his daddy, but it must get lonesome out here. On the other hand, it might be that Jesse liked running the show alone. Not an unattractive prospect.

I missed Daddy Mayhall, or rather missed those large, loud dinners we used to have in our Chicago days, what seemed the confusion of a table crowded with people, the effect due mostly to his booming presence. There was always real talk, work talk. Was Douglas going to take that teaching job in up-state New York? Could he move from there if he didn't get tenure, or wanted a research institution later? What exactly was standout about this brain stuff he was cutting his rats up to study? What was his particular take on it? Who else was working on it? Real talk at least about Douglas's work, if not about mine. But crumbs can seem a loaf, depending on where you come from. In those days, I was grateful enough just to eat at the table of scholarship.

I'd joined the family looking like the kind of girl you saw in films of that era in jeans with a baseball cap turned back-ward, before that was the fad, a mop of curly, unruly hair sticking out, looking as if she hung out with her older brother and his chums waiting for a chance to play shortstop on their team. Small wonder Daddy never addressed me as a graduate student.

On the other hand, at my parents' house, the outside world was a minimal construct. My mom, Mabel, kept brown 'n' serve rolls in her flower-painted breadbox and Sara Lee cake in her aluminum cake tin. On the slightest pretext, she showed you how if you mixed a little Durkee's with tartar sauce you got remoulade and if you mixed a little chopped sweet pickle and catsup with the Hellmann's you got Thousand Island. Dip the tops of tear-apart rolls in melted margarine and they tasted homemade. You had to know the tricks, she said. In my view all her tricks took twice as long, were twice as difficult, and cost at least double just doing the thing from scratch. But scratch, she used to say, was for grannies, was from the old days.

My dad, Marnie Palmer—Round Rock's favorite pharmacist—did pretty much the same at his job, mixing up ingredients from his shelves or, essentially, just transferring capsules and powders from the manufacturer's to his containers. But, he said, it took a lot of reading to do it right, being as how it was his duty to warn his customers on the subject of side effects, about which they were totally unaware and about which the medical profession was indifferent, if not callous.

Alchemists, both of them, trying to spin gold into flax. To make a silk purse into a sow's ear. Me.

"Listen, you two," Jesse said, after she'd handed us bagged lunches to go, and got us settled with glasses of iced tea. "I thought, since now—" She set out a big manila envelope, settling it halfway between Douglas and me on the scarred wooden table. She was in cutoffs and tennis shoes and a big flopping shirt that must have been Daddy's in her former life. She took a breath and started again. "I need to unload a bit of excess real estate on you, as long as you're down in these parts and we don't have to traffic in attorneys and language nobody can understand, or deal with fees nobody can pay."

It took me a moment to understand what Jesse was offering us. The summer place on Sanibel Island, a wildlife haven on Florida's west coast. It had been Daddy's, theirs, when I married into the family. Had been a vacation place for all of us later, when the children were babies, then toddlers. Daddy had put up hammocks and set out binoculars and field guides. Jesse had done crab claws and boiled shrimp.

Douglas and I had never been there alone. It had no ghosts. The rooms held no scraps of fights or hurts or regrets or untranslated requests and refusals. It was a family place, but we'd been there only as part of Daddy Mayhall's family.

Tears welled up in my eyes at the gesture. And at Jesse's perception. She must have smelled trouble between Douglas and me the instant we'd pulled into her gravel drive at dawn. "Jess—" I said, at a loss.

"Hush. I want you to have it, you two. All I've done is rent it out since Daddy died. I'm deeding it right this Texas minute. Down the road, you might want to pass it on to that boy of yours, who might like a place to dry his bones when he comes up out of those caves of his. Meantime, it's yours. I have got the tenants out, and have got you three sets of keys and a packet of maps which don't make any sense until you've already got lost a couple of times, because the scale of miles is about one inch to one inch and that throws you off, when you're used to Texas maps. But it'll all come back to you; you've been there enough." She tied her rust and gray hair off her neck with a red bandanna.

What a needed, timely gift. Douglas and I in our old Victorian home in the chill, hilly Alleghenies were crushing one another with silence. Here was an alternative—some breathing room. I looked at him, but he was bent over the papers, as if examining them.

"I think you're crazy not to stay there half the year yourself," I said. "You love Sanibel."

"Crazy ever to go back," Jesse said. "Wild mares couldn't drag me. Florida? To do the arts with the beige-hairs and give myself skin cancer with the retirees? I'm too old to be with old folks. Anyway, they don't have any decent animals down there. Mini-poos only. Hear me? It's yours."

"Oh, Jesse—" I said. "Thanks."

Douglas turned over the deed, tossed the keys up, and

caught them. His face sagged. "You take it," he said to me, pushing the envelope and maps in my direction.

Daddy Mayhall's widow, to indicate the matter was settled, picked up the San Antonio paper, grazing the headlines, exclaiming, "Would you take a look at this? A contractor is selling bulletproof shields for homes to cut down on drive-by shootings. What next?"

I remembered that she used to read the paper aloud to her dogs and cats, talk to them about the news of the day. "Look at this, Hildy, you are in mortal danger, here, girl." And I wondered who she talked to now, now that tending the territory took all her attention. Maybe she asked the slow-moving, dreamy fed cattle from Planet Cow what she should do about her one remaining stepchild.

2

It was dark and cold when we plunged into the upstate countryside. By the time we'd climbed to Mead's Mill and its university on the hill, land sloping to Canada in our rear-view mirror, the snowstorm we'd been racing from the Syracuse airport hit full force. Snow falling on snow already packed, unshovelled, mountainous. Turning past Chapel Corners and down our street, Douglas cursed. Our driveway lay buried, waist high. He would have to park the car on the street tonight, and hope for the town's forbearance. Tomorrow he would call the fire department and pay them to front-end load a channel through the drifts.

Had I been driving, I would have turned and headed back.

Douglas began to unload the car, but I couldn't move. The night was white already, visibility a foot, a face. It reminded me of the blizzard that hit the first year we came to this seventeenth-century faux British countryside. Douglas was interviewing for a job; he was the top biology candidate. They wanted a brain man. Word came down it was pro forma; he had it if he wanted it. We were married, in love, thrilled, about to begin a new life. To have at least one real job between us.

Someone on the welcoming committee lent me a sheepskin coat, leather on the outside, thick wool on the inside, and a pair of boots, also lined with sheepskin. Everywhere we went, Douglas introduced me to his colleagues, to his future department chair, the dean, "This is my wife, Nan. She's a naturalist in her own right." That being his well-meaning assessment of my having ended up with a passion for paleontology but no Ph.D.

Chilled to the bone, waiting for another member of the welcoming committee to pick me up for dinner, I'd stepped out into the middle of the street, this very same street, and raised my arm. It was almost a whim, almost atavistic. "Taxi," I'd called. "Taxi." Longing for who we were, for our days so freshly left. Having some idea that if there was this much frigid air and heaped snow, then it must be Chicago. You went out into the street and raised your arm and there was a cab. Warm interior, voluble driver, all destinations known in advance, nothing left to chance.

I'd stood that way, tears starting to make cold, straight lines down my cheeks. Stupid, it was, stupid. I'd thought: You jerk, hailing a cab. All the while knowing in my bones, as if it was a certainty carried by the north wind itself, that it was always going to be like this. Douglas starting out on some new venture, another rise in the academic world, and me, in the street, arm raised, going nowhere.

As if a temptation sent by fate, a beat-up yellow car had rounded the corner and pulled to a stop. The driver, a preppie in whatever uniform predated J. Crew, jeans, sweater, parka, had opened the door, made a wide grin, and called to me, "Need a ride?"

What I remembered now, as Douglas dragged bags from the trunk, was the force of my desire to climb in that yellow car and go. "Where to?" he would have asked. "Anywhere. Let's go," I would have answered. And we would have driven to California, to Alaska (dressed for it), to a ranch in Montana. More likely, to Chicago itself, arriving like country people in our muddy car, staring at the tall buildings (not as tall as now, of course), feeling that bitter wind off the lake, laughing at being in the city, runaways together. Using up the woman's traveller's checks, the boy's tank of gas. Saying: Where to now?

Teachers told you that in a dozen years all this, your current mess, would be forgotten. But that wasn't true. You recalled certain times with every fiber of your hands and feet and face: they were dyed into you, indelible.

Now, back here again, standing out in the cold night, with its special rural upstate outdoor smell, surrounded by the unchanged and unchanging muted pastel-painted homes, the cracked small-town sidewalks buried by an avalanche of snow, I could still see the look on that young man's face. Could see the friendly gesture of the flung-open car door, hear the Midwest sturdiness of his voice. And, most of all, feel my terrible longing to get in that yellow car and ride as far as it would take me.

Stepping out into the street, I waved my hand in front of my face, brushing away the falling snow, brushing away the years. Wanting to go back and pick up what I'd left behind. Tears coursing down my icy cheeks, I called out. "Taxi—"

"What are you doing out there?" Douglas yelled. "You'll freeze to death."

"Taxi—" The tears were sticking to my skin.

He grabbed my fingers, wrapping them in his warm woolen gloves. "Nan," he said. "Come in. We're home. Come inside."

☙   ⓖ   ☙

I rubbed my hands together over the warming burner before I put a pan of water on for tea, already being coffeed out. I'd planned to pack away our winter clothes when we got back. Now I was rooting around in the front closet for the heavy gear. By now, you'd think I'd know.

In wool trousers over tights, a down vest and jacket over a sweater, knit hat, and lined gloves, I looked out the window. The wind was blowing sideways, almost directly horizontal. I added a muffler. Had my tea standing up and snug, needing to warm my insides. I was going to pick up the mail that would be waiting at the post office, sorted and rubber-banded. And that meant having to explain to the woman behind the counter where my husband and I had been. In cold climates the locals see every foray out as a trek with sled and sled dogs, using up vital supplies—prodigal and dangerous.

It took an eternity to go out in such weather, especially when your children were small. You bundled each one in a snowsuit which turned them into round balls, you hunted for mittens, for hats with earflaps, you got yourself into warm gear, grabbed the keys, went back for change. Everyone damp with heat by the time you hit the frigid air. And what on earth did people do up here in real emergencies? A child swallowed something, a hot-water heater blew up. By the time you got feet into boots, poked hands in gloves, covered tender cheeks, whole categories of catastrophes could have taken place. I used to feel lucky we had fared so well.

I left a note on my son Bert's answering machine. Pleased to hear his voice say, "Neither Alison nor Bert is here; if you'd like . . ." Glad that the girlfriend, also a diver, was still in the picture. I had called not to talk about the transplant party in Houston, but to say that perhaps I would be coming to Florida, though not his part of it, before too long.

In the street, I kept my head down, my hands in my pockets. I didn't mind it really; my blood had thickened in a quarter of a century, or near enough.

The woman in the post office commented, "You been gone half a week. Looks like you brought the bad weather back with you."

"We went to a—tribute for my husband's preacher," I told her.

"Must've been some party, to go all that way."

"It was," I said, peeling off my gloves to take the mail. "We had a big Texas barbeque and everybody came."

And then here I was, back home, still in my Klondike clothes, on my own, Douglas having already slogged up the hill to school, a retreat provided by his job and salary.

Either I would go see my friend Doris, or I would take off the vest, jacket, wool pants, boots, gloves, scarf, thermal headband. Strip down to my red thermal T-shirt and my red snuggy tights. More and more I was wearing red, to lift my spirits.

I climbed the stairs to Bethany's room. Trying to deal with the fact that I was no more or less employed, no more or less involved in studying the world, because she was gone. She had not had her mother's trouble getting herself a field. She had the young person's confidence that of course you could get paid for doing what you wanted. She'd been good at English; she'd been a runner. In my day, that wouldn't have added up to a summer job. But such were her expectations, and such was today's world, that she had both job plans and study plans: sports reporting, the physiology of female athletes. Track and field, swimming, those events pitting the body against time, starting with the summer and winter Olympic tryouts. She'd made the horizon appear unlimited. The degree to which I'd let her open-ended future be mine was not to my credit.

Her room was now a guest room, for those visitors who did not know the story; we hadn't left it a shrine, the way you saw those dreadful rooms in films. Still, whenever I rounded the corner of the second-floor landing, I could see her dart through her doorway, in pajamas with feet in them, holding a teddy bear, dressed for Halloween as a football player, in her track shorts and jersey, holding a medal. Somewhat like her daddy, in that she was a plain child with a solemn face who grew up and bloomed into someone graceful and fair.

Our last real talk had been one of those painful exchanges that mark being kin. I'd looked around her sunny, cluttered room, a student's room, and wondered how she could bear to be still here, living with her family when there was no need to. How could she not want to pack her belongings in some knapsack and climb the world?

"What're you trying to do, Mom, kick me out of the nest?" she'd asked, making a little grin to soften her words. She was in her nightgown; we were saying good night. "I mean, that's the fifth time since graduation you've asked me what my plans are."

"I just thought," I answered lamely, "you'd want to go." At her age, in her place, I'd have been beyond frantic to leave home, to put all possible distance between me and the morass of my parents' shortsightedness. I couldn't understand how she, so independent and so capable, whose sights glimpsed such a distant horizon, didn't long to set her footprints on a broader trail.

"You going to rent out our rooms?" She'd looked wistfully down the hall toward where her brother used to live. My daughter the peacemaker who didn't like discord, trying to make a joke, trying to understand her mother.

"You know better—" I shook my head and grew silent, aware that it should seem a compliment that this girl becoming a woman wanted to linger awhile.

I watched her brush her hair and wondered if some boy, some man, had been with her. That, also, seemed foreign to me. That she could come down to breakfast still in her terry cloth robe and eat dry cereal along with her dad, and not feel trapped, not be wild to flee, not be slipping out at least to spend whole nights in someone's arms. Twenty-two? I'd have walked the railroad tracks with a hobo's sack on my back before I'd have lived at home.

"Gee, Mom, if you need a breathing spell, I'll go visit Jesse at the ranch or something." She'd looked up at me from the side of her bed, her scrubbed face trying not to register hurt feelings.

"No, of course—" I don't know what I replied, if anything at all. I recall the frustration that my daughter was feeling evicted when I was trying to give her permission to go her own way. The frustration I felt knowing I should be grateful for what time we had her still at home.

I didn't say, Please stay. I didn't say, Don't go.

                                                   ☙   ⑥   ☙

I'd conceived my firstborn on a warm Indian summer day, in the middle of the afternoon, in what, to me then, seemed as perfect a moment as I could have visualized. Me, lifted from my work by her daddy's arms, much like the pianist from the stool in the old Tabu perfume ads, the remains of the world's oldest life at my fingertips.

The second week of Douglas's classes at the university on the hill, I set out for the lakes, Great and Finger, which populated my new countryside. A map on the seat beside me, plus coffee tins, newspapers, and disposable diapers for packing, and a set of picks left from my school days. I was heading for a cow pasture and a quarry and a stream along the length of Lake Cayuga. Going to find where my forebears lay in three parts, pressed in the dark shale much as wildflowers are pressed between the pages of a book.

I'd gone slowly out of town, the trees already turning their metallic golds and coppers, past rugby and crew teams warming up, racing up and down the steep hills, along the sidewalks, past the playing fields, racing as if to meet their futures, made impatient by the glorious weather.

I drove a zigzag route of narrow winding country roads from the foothills of the Alleghenies to the Finger Lakes, heading for where my past lay spread out along a creek like a fine picnic for the sampling. This was my first field trip since graduate days; my very first dig alone. But I was on the trail of the same formations that ran from Ohio along the large interlocked lakes; I was on familiar ground.

Going down a dirt road that ran between the highway and the lake, parallel to both, I pulled off onto a quarry's dusty service road, following my map guides, curious, expecting, from my reading, to see a big white dome of salt. Seeing, instead, an immensely vast excavation, forty trucks of various sorts, huge two-story-high trucks, ascending and descending down a series of switchbacks into a gaping tan canyon. I'd learned that early state geologists had found specimens there, on a fault line between formations underlain with salt and shale. But that would have been in an earlier day, on burrow-back, sacks over their saddles.

Heading down the river road again, I passed an abandoned mill beside a rickety-looking bridge, and then, directly on my left, found the stream and small waterfall. And there, just as my field notes promised, an outcropping of Windom shale, soft as Greek pastry, crumbling and flaky at the edges. Dark gray, black where wet from the water, sandy gray when dry, and covered with silt from the quarrying above. And I'd lifted layers of it carefully, thinking of the scientists like myself working in the same formations in Scotland and Wales, kneeling beside their gurgling brooks, removing with care their grayed and graceful crumbling banks. Their hands touching land which had once abutted mine.

Back in our rattling hand-me-down Victorian, I hadn't even stopped to eat but spread my loot on newspapers on the kitchen table. And, as if doing surgery, as if lifting the rib cage off a heart, pulling back a breathing lung, I'd let my eyes grow accustomed to the dark gray remains embedded in the dark gray formation. The fossils appearing to be made of the same material because of course they were: the original creature long ago washed out, with only the replica remaining.

All trilobites, as did this one, *Phacops rana*, occurred in three sections (hence *tri*lobite), something like a crab shell from which the crab has departed. I started with the tails (pygidium), the easiest to see, which looked very much like miniature bats in flight, a center section with two wings. Using a magnifying glass to be sure, and a small pick to ease them out, I slipped five tails onto a sheet of thick white paper and set them carefully aside. Then I went for the midsections, the kite-shaped trunks with their lateral segments the Scots called ribs. It seemed an eternity—a pot of coffee, a trip to pee, two trips to wash the dust from my hands—before I found a head. And so thrilled was I, by this time surrounded by heaps of grungy newspapers covered with damp phyllo dough, that I quite shouted it out loud. "A head!" And it was a complete helmet, its silt-covered, slate-colored Greek statue eyes all there. Rows and rows and rows of tiny, round, compound eyes. The whole able to see in all directions at once, 360 degrees. Why had the trilobite been so farsighted? So ready to view a future which never arrived?

At that moment, Douglas came in and threw his professor's tweedy blue jacket over the back of a nearby kitchen chair. Bending over my shoulder to look.

"Dr. Leakey, I presume?" he said, smiling down on me, careful not to jar the table.

"You may call me Mary," I replied, pleased but wanting to be certain he was referring to the right Leakey.

Then he bent and lifted me from my chair, his arms around me, his mouth finding mine, not minding the thick dust, the bits of black shale, my stained white T-shirt. "Let's make a baby," he said, pulling me by my hand toward the stairs.

That seemed the most grand, the most auspicious start for a child I could imagine. And I willed it to be a girl, born with the mark of science on her brow, our warm blood mingling in her veins.

Here on the floor of the room that would later be hers, we lay down and I locked my legs around him and we let her begin.

☙　⑥　☙

I'm back," I told Doris.

"I'll be right there—" She gave the automatic Best Friend response.

"No, I'll come. I've still got all my gear on. The mail was a bunch of bills. A postcard from Bert saying he's still alive, which isn't quite the casual comment it used to be."

"I was wanting an excuse to have something with grape jelly on it."

"Thanks."

Doris lived past Chapel Corners, up the hill behind the school on Angel Rock Ridge. It was a good walk, good for the rear-end muscles, and I needed that.

We'd met before the Flood it seemed like, literally before our first pregnancies. We were assigned to each other, new members of a covert women's group. I'd been contacted as soon as Douglas arrived on campus. The idea had come, the woman called Winifred had told me confidentially, from her kid brother, at least initially, and then had expanded.

He'd been in their parents' hair in elementary school, nagging for Popsicle money or whatever, and they'd said, "Go open a lemonade stand, why don't you?" Benign summer venture capitalism they recalled from their own childhood. Instead, her brother had opened up a burgeoning playground business called Rent-a-Friend. Figuring, he said, from watching all the moms pick up their kids, that the only things moms cared about was, did you have a friend. For a quarter a week (culled from lunch money) he would present himself as your best friend at car-pool time. Hey, Frank, what's up, what's happening, buddy, see you tomorrow. A slap on the back or a punch to the shoulder, whatever the old-days version of high five was. Mothers flushing with delight that this nice-looking boy had singled out their son, formerly a loner or wimp or bully.

Winifred, my hostess, had said it all came back to her during her first year here as the spouse of an academic, in History. The third time her husband had asked, "Are you making any friends here, honey?" she had wished for her brother's service. And had cooked up the idea of a service of her own. She called it Lemonade Stand.

This is the idea, Winifred told me, over tea in her mauve living room. Your best friend is always on call, day or night, for anything. Your mom is coming, she's there, to bring coffee cake, the kind you "always love." She knows all about you— you supply the bio. You break your leg on this idiot ice up here, she's at the hospital, she brings your husband tuna noodle. You have a supper party, she drags her spouse, who is not in on the secret but who is delighted that she has made a friend and got you invited to dinner with someone who isn't in his department. You do the same for her.

"It doesn't matter whether you actually like one another," the older woman had explained. "This is a service. Although," she'd said firmly, "we find that through the years, naturally, we have mostly bonded with one another by having been in on the inside of one another's lives. When a husband has his affair—my dear, you're so young, what a thing to be speaking of—with some robustly-breasted student, the friend is there for you."

"But," I'd asked, looking around the drafty room the size of a train station, "doesn't everyone already have a friend?"

"We have someone who tends to that," she'd replied.

My Best Friend was, at first, quite a disappointment. Someone I was sure that Douglas would never believe I had picked. Doris was fat, there was no other way to say it, and there was no blame in that—I was certain that if I lived the rest of Douglas's academic life in this frozen, quaint, tiny, steeple-stabbed town, I'd be a tub myself. But Doris was also a non-reader, a non-scholar, and didn't have many interests.

The reason we were paired, we learned later, was that we

were the only two women who did not yet have children. With children and without children being the way that women were divided. On the theory that it was convincing that you'd made friends with the mother of a girl in your daughter's class or on your son's team at school. And, in fact, Doris and I had run into each other shortly after we'd been introduced—in the office of the town's most trusted OB. A logical place, since that meeting really happened and since making babies was clearly on our minds.

Doris had stayed heavy for all the years we'd been in Mead's Mill. But after that first month, the sound of her voice on the phone was a blessing. She always called when she knew Douglas would be home. "It's that friend of yours," he'd say, handing me the phone. "Can't you get her to call you sometime when we're not eating supper? Doesn't she feed that scarecrow of hers?" But he was so obviously pleased that I'd made a friend, that I wasn't going to be lonesome, that I wouldn't grow unhappy—the greatest fear of husbands. We did our assignment well. Appearing whenever kin came, whenever it was time for the surprise party (the big Three-Oh), or the supper party in the backyard, coals charring meat for some new department head or some departing non-tenured friend. We learned to speak a common language: Doris asked after Daddy Mayhall's wife, I asked after Miss Sunshine. References we didn't understand, at first, something like a language immersion course.

On the top of the hill, I stopped for breath under the oldest stand of fir trees. Overcome by affection for those young pregnant women, those young mothers we were. For how innocent we seemed. In retrospect, how safe and tame our lives, even when our husbands had had those affairs, even when some of us retaliated. But nothing cut too deep in those years; nothing was permanent.

The first time Doris called on me for serious help was the year after our husbands got tenure. My Bethany and her David Junior were in kindergarten; I'd had one more, she'd had three.

"Nan? This is Doris."

If it was possible to say that four words sounded like an overdose of sleeping pills or a razor to the wrist, then Doris's did. "I'll be right there," I told her, giving the Best Friend pledge. I grabbed my three-year-old, stuffed him into his snowsuit, checked the stove, found my keys, put on my own winterproof layers.

She was waiting in her overheated lilac and beige sitting room, a puddle of red eyes and wet cheeks. Too dreadful.

"A student?" I asked.

Doris sniffled. "He doesn't love me anymore."

Naturally, I thought, because your body has been to the well four times and David is sleeping with a stranger: you. Why did no one ever reckon with the change that pregnancy made? That any change in the body made? I'd been through the same thing with Douglas; it was the worst fight we'd ever had.

"I'm more myself with her," he had said, hangdog but determined to be truthful. "You're different, Nan. You're somebody else these days. She makes me feel—"

"Of course I am different." We'd been sitting up on the bed, and it did seem he could have told me when we weren't in our night clothes, propped up against pillows on our marriage bed. "I'm not the same because my body had a baby." I kept my voice down, since Bethany was in her crib down the hall.

"I had a baby, too," he said. "You seem to forget she's ours."

"You didn't *have* her, you didn't carry her in your belly space. Your body did not have to mutate and molt. How can you be surprised I'm someone else? All change is information received from the body."

"Dammit, Nan, you spout that whenever—"

"You think the mind sits on its throne and, once developed, sends occasional telegrams to the body."

"I think," he said, shouting, "THAT ISN'T YOUR FIELD."

I felt as though I'd been slapped. *My field.* It was a wonder you were allowed to say I'm hungry or salads are good for you, if you didn't have a degree in biochemistry and perhaps botany. I'd looked down at my fuller breasts, my still-pouchy stomach. I wanted sex all the time in those days, like a grazing animal chewing and chewing. He hadn't liked that either, the almost aimless gnawing quality of it. "You're wrong," I said. "It's just common sense. Think, Douglas. If a person stayed all her—let's say her—life a six-pound fourteen-ounce person, then her mind would stay the mind of a six-pound fourteen-ounce person. All changes that happen to the mind happen BECAUSE THE BODY CHANGES." Now I was shouting, also. "And you've changed, too, Douglas. You've fucked a twenty-one-year-old and you're not the same person you were. Despite all your efforts, despite all your protests, you've changed yourself."

These days, I thought, turning onto Angel Rock Ridge, I would have welcomed such a fight—true words hurled with a heavy hand. Hurtful yet still better than our present silent truce. Anger was the glue that held a marriage together.

"What can I do?" Doris had wept, grape juice and tears staining her housedress.

What indeed? I'd wondered. Run him through with a kitchen knife? Poor gaunt geographer, David Senior, not a likely end for him. Heartburn and heartache would suit him better. I'd patted her swollen knee, aware that young Bert was growing fussy in the too-hot room. "Spicy foods," I declared.

"What?"

"Start with Mexican. Move to East Indian. Then try Szechwan Chinese. The hotter the better. You'll see. The student will be gone by Groundhog Day."

"Really?"

"Lemonade Stand put us together for a reason," I told Doris.

∞   ⑥   ∞

Doris had aged well through the years. Her face was unlined and as pretty as in the bridal photo on her skirted end table. (Doris and David on their wedding day, she wide-eyed in eyelet, a mass of veil, a string of pearls, a white orchid centered in stephanotis, and David a beanpole in a rented tuxedo.) If she hadn't lost any weight, she hadn't gained any either, so that there weren't the wrinkles and stretch lines of constant gaining and losing. She had a dozen catalogues for Large and Real Women to order from now. Attitudes and styles had changed. But it was more than that, really; it was that as we aged, our character got written all over our face, and Doris's sent a good message.

Plus, once-scrawny David Senior was now porky, and so couldn't go on at every meal about how he could eat anything he wanted and never gain an ounce. A geographer who seemed to have swallowed a continent a decade.

"How did it go?" she asked when we were settled with our bagels and grape jelly. Coffee for me, a diet drink for her.

"This heart business is going to tear us apart. Tell me

something new. I feel like I haven't talked about anything else since the wreck—"

"You want to hear about our trip to Mobile?"

"Mightily." Mostly I wanted someone to talk to me about matters not even tangential to my own; I wanted a reminder that there were other solar systems out there, other galaxies of people with kin and backaches and crow's-feet and bank balances and grocery sacks.

"I have to tell you," Doris said, arranging two lilac sofa cushions behind her, tucking up her feet, "we were a hit." Her hair was blunt-cut now, colored a shiny beige, and swung across one cheek. The new look was because David Junior was marrying a girl from Mobile, Alabama, an exotic distant nation to Doris and David.

"No surprise."

"—And it was all because I remembered what you said about the South. How you had to come empty-handed. How it was an insult to arrive with something when you'd been invited over, like you thought your hostess didn't have the taste to already have it or couldn't afford it if she'd wanted it. Boy, that was hard for me, you know it was, just thinking all your life that you're supposed to bring a gift, but we did just that. We walked in the door of her parents' house without a thing in our hands, and I gave her mom that kiss on both cheeks the way you said. And I could see *exactly* what you meant—"

I tried to focus on that living room in Alabama, and not on David Junior, born six weeks after Bethany. A big lump of a good-natured boy, with a brain like a runaway train, who could have hacked his way through all the secrets of the Pentagon except that that wouldn't have been polite. Going down there to meet his girlfriend's family.

"—I mean everything was this coral and orange and

bridal white, all the flowers and her dress and even the dessert, the whole business. And the only other people there from up East were the best man's family, and, the way we might have, they did just the wrong opposite. They came in with that bottle of red wine and a bunch of silver-wrapped flowers and you could see that her mom wanted to throw both right in the trash. So I owe you one again—"

It was unbearable to think that my daughter would never make that trip to meet her in-laws. That there would not be those pictures sitting on some son's mother's end table, the bride and groom cutting the cake. Or whatever the new way was, whatever lighthearted ceremony Bethany might have come up with, whatever casual way of tying herself to the man who had her love. I tried a bite of bagel but couldn't get it down. Doris, trying to help, was only rubbing salt in the wound.

"My mom was always insulted when people at the door poked things at her," I said.

"You lost your parents young, same as I did. The Alchemists." Doris made her Best Friend reference.

"Going in your sixties doesn't seem so young anymore."

"Nan, I'm sorry."

"No, please. It's me."

"How was Daddy Mayhall's wife?"

"She gave us the keys to the place on Sanibel Island."

"Lucky you. Just thinking of Florida in this blizzard gives me a suntan. Will you go down?"

"Maybe."

"You know if I can do anything, Nan, any single thing at all. I still owe you one I can never repay. You know, for that time—"

David Senior had been on Maalox ever since the spicy

foods were put into effect. That brought a smile. "I was think-ing about that, the old days. When that seemed the very worst thing that could happen."

"I honestly thought you might run off with that guy from Chicago."

"I would have run off with Chicago if I could have, but not him. Anyway, who owes who for that one?"

Only Doris knew I'd had that affair—probably entered into to get revenge against Douglas for his. Although I thought at the time, and still do if I think of it, that it was more a wish to escape this village in the foothills, this campus-locked community.

He was a stranger—rare enough right there—visiting a colleague here while his wife was with her dying mother in Ohio; I was his dinner partner. Douglas was giving a paper at a conference.

Afterward, I wasn't sure which had come first, the de-sire to sleep with him or a longing to be in the Windy City. "What do you do?" I'd asked him, knowing that wasn't the thing to say anymore, now that you were supposed to let a man just be, now that you could safely ask most women, What do you do?

"Nothing, in a sense," he answered. He had very dark eyes. Chicago was a city of many backgrounds, but he seemed foreign to me. Not ethnic but foreign, whatever the difference was. I noticed his white-on-white shirt and his cuffs with their thick stiffened folds.

"Me, too," I said. "I'm not someone in my own right." I'd laughed. By that time, I was confident of my looks. The babies had filled me out in some inner way. I wasn't a girl anymore, wasn't hollow, wasn't greedy for more and more and more. And, vexingly, I now seemed "the same" again to Douglas. But that was an illusion. Looking at the tomboy school-days photos of Nan Palmer, I knew I was someone else.

He'd laughed, too, and then and there put his hand on my shoulder, as if looking past me at someone down the table.

I'd wondered what the woman did in reply, then turned to him and touched my fingertip to his lips. "You've got a bit of cream," I said.

He'd called the next morning before my alarm went off, before the children were even awake for school, and if he hadn't, I'd have thrown myself in front of the snowplow. "Yes," I said as soon as I lifted the receiver.

Doris had taken the children while Douglas was out of town, with instructions to say that I was sick as a dog, something I'd eaten at the dinner, not to call.

His name was Joseph Nancarrow. The building he worked in was on Michigan Avenue; I recognized the address. What he'd meant by doing nothing, he said, was that most days he didn't. Architects, he said, were the most visible and also invisible of people. You could go in any city and ask, Who did that building? And your guide would say, Someone famous, I don't know.

"What I meant by doing nothing was nothing," I told him. Thrilled to be with someone who hadn't done a longitudinal study of me, who wasn't going to say: You've changed, you didn't used to eat tomatoes that way.

We'd hardly left the bed. Joseph's wife, he said, was never gone, never let him out of her sight. She had no interests, was always free to travel with him, if it hadn't been for her sick mother—

The last night, we'd looked out at the dark lake through the dark plate glass of his high-rise, the wind buffeting the building so hard it seemed to sway. Joseph said that he wasn't

foreign at all. That he was from the Midwest. I knew that did
not mean that he'd grown up in Wideroad, Illinois, Bigriver,
Ohio, or Cornfield, Kansas, but that he hadn't gotten his education at the Ivies, Chicago, or California.

"Will I see you again?" I asked.

"That depends on my mother-in-law," he'd said, serious.

And as far as I knew, she was still alive some dozen
years later.

That was the only time I called on Doris. When we heard
about the wreck this fall, when it was something that sliced
our lives apart, there had been no favor to ask.

She poured me another cup of coffee, weak the way non-
drinkers made it, but hot. Her kindly face had puckers of concern. "I do have some news," she said, her tone tentative.

"Good?"

"In a way." She tugged at her purple sweats, got settled.
"After you lost—her, I got to thinking. About what were you
going to do, you know, and then I thought, what am *I* going
to do when this last one graduates from high school this
year—and, please Artemis, none of them will come home
to live—and David Senior keels over from Geographers' syndrome. And I couldn't for the life of me think. I mean if there
was nothing to do here *now*, I told myself, why did I think
there's suddenly going to be something to do here *then*? You
know what I did? You don't, because I haven't really talked to
you for moons and moons, just to talk. I started playing the
stock market."

"With what, if I may ask."

"Oh, it really didn't take all that much money. I took what
I'd ratted away for a sunny day, and plunked it all down. I
bought thirty stocks, one or two little shares of each. And now
I get to follow them all. Every morning I trudge up and get
USA Today as soon as they stuff the papers in that wire cage,

and then I come home and have to look up each one and see if it's up or down. It takes half the morning, plus then I fret all day about the ones that are down half a point, and should I sell them and buy more of the ones that are up a half point. I talk to a stockbroker in Syracuse, and he says business is slow-times-slow, so he doesn't mind advising. I know he's probably reading off some flyer on his desk while he's having a Danish, but I don't care."

I was charmed by the idea. It was brilliant. What could you do snowed in up here that wasn't drink yourself to death or eat yourself porcine? Paint by numbers, do thousand-piece jigsaw puzzles. "Maybe Lemonade Stand ought to start an investment group," I suggested.

Doris beamed and leaned back on the lavender pillows. "I already thought of that. I talked to Winifred, and she said she'd pass the idea around. I said that the concept of Lemonade Stand was okay in its day, but that not only did husbands not care anymore if you had friends, probably your own mother didn't either. Husbands just wanted to know if you could make ends meet and maybe squirrel a little away. I suggested we call it Paper Route, and she liked that a lot."

"—And did you call Miss Sunshine and tell her about it?" Doris's sister was her only remaining family member, and about as supportive as a flat tire.

"Miss Sunshine is on lithium and Prozac and Ritalin, although only sequentially she says. The trouble is remembering when to take which." Doris slapped her hand on her lilac knee. "How about that?"

Siblings were a complex business. Not that I'd had first-hand experience, although my mom used to say that surely all her early miscarriages should add up to one offspring and I should consider myself the baby of the family. But I was thinking of Bert. I had no idea what he was feeling about

Bethany. He didn't seem to come up for air anymore. I didn't know if he was trying to burst his lungs or simply keep his head under water till he was able to deal with the absence of his sister. I bit my lip.

"What?" Doris asked. "Nan, what? Did I say something wrong?"

"No." I closed my eyes, then opened them again, trying to get a grip. I tried to let my shoulders relax, my mind go blank. "I'm sorry," I said. "All roads lead to home."

3

The snow was gone, and spring hit as it always did in the foothills of the Alleghenies: swift and sunny. The air turned fresh and fragrant; shoots poked through the slush, turning overnight into flowers. The playing fields came alive with students kicking their way to goals or bases or punts, jerseys torn, knees muddy. And then the runners, filling their lungs and stretching their calf muscles, suddenly everywhere, arriving overnight like the crocus and iris and alpine gentian, the bluebells and columbine. Winter sports, ice hockey, and cross-country skiing, gone from their heads.

"Let's have some people over," Douglas said at the breakfast table. He was finishing his Grape-Nuts with a sprinkling of bran on top and a banana, while I ate my Pepperidge Farm skinny toast. The world of plenty was divided into those who liked their grain with milk and those who liked it with butter.

"Who?" I poured myself a cup of fresh Braun-ground

and -dripped coffee, exactly strong enough and hot enough, in my favorite cup: thick with a black-and-white cow and letters which said EAT CHICKEN.

"We haven't had people since—the fall," he said. "Everyone had us then. We owe everyone."

That was true. We had been fed and fed after the wreck. Buffets and sit-downs, tables at all the local inns. Dinners on the hill, in the hollow, outside town past Devil's Elbow Bend. How else to offer sympathy in the bleak, cold stretches of the holiday months?

"Let's do," I said, looking out the kitchen window at the runners.

As I watched, a steady stream of female students sailed past on the sidewalk, as if every coed on campus had been assigned to jog past the Mayhall house, a steady stream like a movie clip over and over and over. I could see our daughter. Her length of straight fair hair rising and falling in a rhythm that echoed her stride. She had on leg weights, small ones, Velcroed around her white athletic socks. She had a certain thrust to her heels and push with her knees which set her apart from the other runners. She wore a sweatband, terry cloth, white, on her forehead. Her once plain, now radiant face was set in total concentration.

I used to worry Bethany would overdo, pull a muscle. You read about the tennis players who put themselves out of commission for a season or more. But she'd wrinkle her lightly tanned skin, look out at me with her daddy's blue, nearsighted eyes, and say, "Oh, don't be a Nanny Mom." Her term for hovering. The same thing she said when I fretted aloud about Bert, his dangerous dives, the fact that we hadn't heard from him in two weeks or more. "Don't be a Nanny Mom," she'd say. "They're *his* lungs."

"Who, then?" I asked Douglas, taking my plate to the

sink, turning my back to the window. At that moment, I was able to remember perhaps twelve people in the entire community, the same twelve we'd seen every weekend for years. At every on-campus lecture or colloquy. At everyone's home for welcomes and farewells. But he was right, of course; it was our turn.

"Let's think about it." He sounded glad, cheered.

We were both dressed in dug-out-of-boxes spring warm-up shorts, navy with drawstring waists, looking like members of the same team. Together, we cleared the kitchen and began to follow each other through the house, by instinct, as though turning into any room alone might prove unnerving. I thought Douglas seemed unaware of this, the way a scientist in the lab doesn't notice what the white Norways are doing, for concentrating on the experiment's aim.

I sat on the side of the claw-footed tub while he shaved. "I'd like to have Winifred," I offered, beginning our guest list. Lemonade Stand's leader was a recent widow. "We haven't had her over since her husband died."

He nodded, then proposed the friend he played handball with on Tuesdays and Thursdays. His wife was a friend of Winifred's, though younger, he reminded me. Yes, I agreed, that was good. And—he sliced away a stripe of shaving cream—the new man in his department, who was tenure-track, or would be if Biology could get the university on the hill to come up with the money, and who had not been given a proper welcome in the fall. Good idea, I agreed. He added Bethany's favorite teacher, a woman in English, sans husband at this point. The table was filling.

We stopped in the doorway of Bethany's room. I had filled it with furniture from the attic, returning a sit-down vanity with mirror that she had banished in high school. Bought new red-checked bedding. Repainted the walls. It was a lost cause;

the room was a room not at home in the house. A guest room. I would like to have given it—the entire room, removed it from the walls of the house—to the Next-to-New shop. Or sent it to a shelter for the homeless in some city. What could you do with an off-limits room in your own house? We were not going to ride Exercycles in there; I was not going to sew. Douglas was not going to move his computer in. We couldn't even send company up to throw their coats on the bed. Some-one had suggested we bring in an exchange student, so that it belonged to a fresh face. Someone else offered to donate her mother-in-law.

In reflex, Douglas touched the notches in the doorframe where we had measured the children year by year, our son's height finally passing our daughter's when he was fourteen and she was sixteen.

Only seven years ago.

Douglas put on his leather shoes in Bert's room, where I kept my typewriter and correspondence on a carved-up desk at which our son had studied. His presence was here, but not in such a painful way. I could see him at the desk, looking up at his dad, raising his voice, insisting, "I am not a recreational diver. I am a scientific diver. Call me a breathing support sys-tem if that will make you happy, Dad." Douglas leaving the room, passing me in the hall and reporting he thought his son was growing gills.

He stood and buttoned his shirt and tucked it in. Blue-striped. He wore it or one like it most days on the campus. He had on his teaching trousers. He looked around, not seeing. "We've an extra woman?" he calculated. "I'd like to ask the guy from Ithaca who's helping on this twin study. Bring in someone from the outside."

I was glad enough if he was back on the twin study, back with his correlations. Although the premise—that the concordance rate for coronary disease in identical twins had something to do, not with their identical predisposition to high blood pressure or serum cholesterol, but with something in how the mind organized itself to handle stress—seemed to me all wrong. All studies of identical twins seemed wrong to me. The people doing them were looking at their theory and not the data. (Not that the brain scientist, Douglas, having gone to private school, was, himself, naturally, actually going out and examining five thousand pairs of identical twins in Buffalo and Cedar Rapids and Montpelier and San Diego. That went without saying. He was, I supposed you could say, a theoretical biologist.)

I sat on the side of Bert's bed and tied my Reeboks. "Why don't you guys see the obvious?" I asked, arguing out of reflex. "Identical twins turn out alike because they both look exactly alike so people treat them exactly alike. They both marry girls named Shirley because girls named Shirley marry boys who look like that. And because they're treated exactly alike, they respond exactly alike. The information they've received through their bodies tells their minds—"

"Nan, dammit—" Douglas raised his hand as if to slam it down on the desk and shower the floor with my unanswered condolence letters and unpaid bills. But then he dropped his arm and turned away. He wouldn't fight. He had turned the other cheek so much lately his face now seemed chapped from good intentions.

But if he didn't respond, then I couldn't have my say. Couldn't tell him that even if it wasn't my field, I might still have opinions about twins. People didn't stop noticing the world and putting things together, trying to make sense of it all—and wasn't that what science did?—just because they had failed to stake a claim to one narrow strip of academic arcana.

He followed me into our bedroom. Although quilts were still piled at the foot of the bed, Appalachian quilt-makers' finest, not yet packed away for mild weather, the flannel sheets were in the laundry and had been replaced by creamy percales that seemed a luxury in themselves. Our birds, which had come back from wherever they spent our bitter winters, mixed their loud calls with the student sounds out the window.

"Do you feel I've kept you from your work, is that it?" Douglas sat on the high bed, hands flat on his knees. This was his morning to catch up on correspondence at home, to go to school late. Out of habit, he looked at his watch anyway.

"Why are you asking me this now?" I folded a favorite quilt, a star-patterned one that Bethany had miscalled "star-padded" as a child.

"Why now?" Douglas looked out the window at the bird feeder. "Guilt that wants a home, I guess." He ran his hands over his eyes, as if to wipe away his good looks, like rain on a windshield. It was a gesture I knew well; I'd seen him before an auditorium of like-minded scholars, wiping his face, clearing his throat, trying to be again that scrawny boy with the eyeglasses.

How honest he always was, how truthful to the best of his ability. And such a contradiction, as all of us were. A biologist who kept a mentor's words above his desk—EMBODIMENT IMPOSES INELUCTABLE LIMITS—yet who, in truth, did not feel that his own body was anything but a counterfeit presentation, an obstacle that his mind had to signal past, semaphoring to passersby, Hey, I'm in here.

"No," I told him. And as best I could manage, I was speaking the truth. We'd made a deal. Every couple was a compromise. The spouses' trade-off. "You have no cause to feel guilty, Douglas."

"The survivor always does," he said.

I followed him downstairs, stopping at his study door. I could tell, from the tilt of his reading glasses, from the hunch of his shoulders, that he was writing the preacher. From the manner in which he stiffened, hearing me behind him. The idea of it drove me crazy, those letters. Especially so when, to the best of my knowledge, he had never written a single letter to his own son since Bert went off to Florida State. Not one.

Douglas had defended himself in the past to me. "The boy knows I don't write letters," he'd say. "Come on, our son is not much of a correspondent himself. It's the E-mail age," he'd say, "the fax age." "But," I'd argue back, "those messages don't require the receiver to be there." "As opposed to a letter?" he'd counter. "A letter is personal," I tried to explain.

One foot in the hall, hand on the knob, I said, "You're writing the Reverend Clayton."

"Was I supposed to clear that with you?" He didn't turn around.

"Why, Douglas? Why again?"

"I want him to know he has my support."

You want to hear, I thought, that he puts his hand on his chest every morning in bed, his frail bony chest, his head propped on three rosebud-stitched pillowcases, and says, "We're okay, Bethany girl, we're hanging in there."

"I'm signing both our names," Douglas said, his voice low.

I let myself out the kitchen door, wearing only a light jacket, heading past the small campus lake, out to the turn-around at Devil's Elbow Bend. Students running all around me like an honor guard. A kindly corps.

            ☙   ⑥   ❧

The supper party—dinner party as they said in the East, but childhood language remained—went well. It should have patched up things between us. Douglas had put together friends who would break the silence that hung in our house like icicles; I had the pleasure of gathering together people who were not kin, in getting loose from the slipknot of family. Deciding that must have been the appeal of the early church suppers—congregation-wide gatherings which let you get your mind off what was going on under your roof, behind your closed doors at home.

Although my house was never going to be the kind that implied generations of female food preparers—no cake tin, no flour bin, no teapot with tea cozy—for this particular spring evening we'd chosen, I did the very best I knew how to make it healing for us as well as inviting for our guests.

First, flowers everywhere. I'd gone on foot down our street, Stone Hollow Road, to Fern the Florist's and gotten an armload of yellow lilies and brown iris, velvety ones the color of the living room walls. (Actually, as everyone in Mead's Mill knew, Fern ran the travel agency and her husband Fred ran the florist shop, but "Fern" was a better name for flowers than "Fred.") Then I went back in the car, and got branches of freesia and a couple of stems of forsythia.

I made lists and changed my mind; worked out menus and started over from scratch. I made everything take more time than it needed to. All of it was good for my spirits. I liked going in and out of shops, circling the green with an armload, going back for one more item, looking in all the windows filled with the chickens and eggs of Easter.

Chapel Corners, the square where all the shops clustered, was ringed with churches. There was one Methodist (which Douglas and I did not attend), one Roman Catholic (which Doris and David Senior did not attend), one Congregational (Winifred's), one Presbyterian (by tradition, the denomination of the college president), and all the rest were Baptist. All of which, like eager aging genealogists, traced their antecedents back to the Anabaptists who so pestered the Puritans. Since most of the faculty didn't know the ins and outs of which was which, and since most darkened the doors of churches only for student weddings and parents' weekend, they were generally referred to as Creation, Original, Ancient, and Elderly Baptist. But despite such levity, all seemed to flourish in this little valley they had settled.

Douglas took charge of the wine, and he made much of his selections, making several forays out to the convenient liquor store and the rather distant "good" liquor store. He asked my advice. French? Italian? Californian? Something rarer? He asked what else he should get and whether the martini had indeed come back, and if so, back even to our insular community.

We fussed with place cards and decided against them. With dripless candles in holders versus the kind you floated in water. Debates which were a first in the twenty-five years of our marriage, a marriage used to casseroles, stews, plates before the fire. We agreed on Mozart, turned low.

We spent considerable time arranging a cleared space on the kitchen counter for the presents of home-preserved chutneys and jams sure to be presented at the door, and I set two heavy vases filled with water by the front door, for a bouquet of mixed host-gift blooms.

Everyone returned the favor of our eager preparation. They arrived on time, some even early; they dressed up. Wearing their light, bright party clothes in celebration of the fine weather. No heavy navy jackets on the men; no black tube dresses with black leotards on the women. They came in crayon shades, festive after two gray seasons back to back. Festive because Douglas and Nan were at last opening their doors again.

I liked both the solo women, one an old and one a new acquaintance. Winifred, Lemonade Stand's leader, now in her mid-seventies and quite a stately woman, appeared in a long apple-green dress with matching glove-leather slippers. Bethany's favorite teacher, Carole, had the crisp, sharp edges of those who taught English: flared shoulders on her Popsicle-orange dress, silver belt buckle centered below a row of silver buttons, silver triangles intersecting the air below her small earlobes. Brisk and cool, she hadn't seemed someone that our daughter would take to, but there was a dogged quality to her, an insistence on doing things over right, however many tries it took, that Bethany had understood and learned from. Douglas and I had included her in the family graduation ceremony last spring. She sat with us at the memorial service here, after the Texas funeral.

During the visiting time before supper, over wine, I talked with Winifred about Doris's investment-club idea. We'd chosen the small cocoa velvet sofa, out of earshot. "Paper Route," we said, and smiled at one another.

"I'd thought of Shoe Shine," Winifred confided, glad to be praising the enterprise of my Best Friend. "This name is better."

Sitting close so she could hear me, I could see the older woman had applied faint green eyeshadow the color of her dress. But so discreet. Turning her hazel eyes green.

When Douglas's handball friend came up, with his wife who knew Winifred (she was a recently added member of Lemonade Stand), I moved over to talk to Carole. I thought it might be awkward—we'd kept Bethany from the room so far—but the young woman was direct even in her grief, and asked interested, fairly clinical questions about the donor-recipient party, in so even a tone I was giddy with relief. I even got up my nerve to mention to her that I'd broached the idea of watching a transplant with the heart surgeon, Angleton.

"That would be enlightening," Carole said, seeming to mean it. She was sipping white wine and I saw her fingernails were angled, too. "I bet that would be good for you to do, Nan. I truly mean it."

Then, for that generosity, I introduced her to the visiting biologist from Ithaca, the one doing the twin study with Douglas, having previously noted that he didn't have a ring on. He looked to be in his forties, a respectable decade older than she, and said his name was Jay. (I'd thought Douglas called him Hay, a historic name, but was apparently mistaken.) I liked men who wore mustaches and met your eyes; perhaps Bethany's empathic young teacher did also.

"What's your connection with these two?" I heard him ask her. But then Douglas, who had been tending the wine and serving gin to those who wanted it in our silver highballs (really julep cups, a wedding present), came over and usurped his colleague, taking him away to discuss the twin study. And, perhaps, in order not to have to explain about his daughter to someone new.

After a bit, I joined the men, slipping an arm around my husband's waist lightly, demonstrating that we were a couple but that I was not interrupting. Douglas wore a yellow silk shirt, open at the neck, and pleated lightweight slacks. I'd worn my loose yellow pajama pants and an overblouse with short sleeves and scoop neck. We were still on the same team. I'd tamed my mop of hair, putting a gold comb to hold it in place, and released my feet from their snow boots into slim spring slippers.

The men, it turned out, were not discussing the twin experiments on reaction to stress after all. Instead, they were talking depression. Whether too much noradrenaline could cause abnormal function just as easily as too little. Whether (a biogenic amine hypothesis) the brain of the depressed person was failing to deliver a sufficient amount of reward. Could this process that resulted in insufficiency be inherited?

I was touched.

How like Douglas this was. Depressed himself until he could hardly pull on his socks in the morning, what did he do? He brought someone down to talk about the biochemistry of depression. Providing a way for him to stand here and talk about his slump for close to an hour. To deal with what it felt like—What's the point anymore?—while keeping it safely within his fenced field. Oh, Douglas, I thought, how hard it is for you.

In this mood of sudden compassion, I served the meal. It was sit-down, since there were only eight of us. Dinner at eight for eight. Such a long time since we'd done this, but what a healing meal. I hadn't done anything fancy. A cold watercress soup to celebrate the balmy weather, served in the rest of the julep cups. A Virginia ham, which I'd ordered. A squash soufflé and a salad of garden greens. For dessert—which was all most of the guests cared about, since bitter weather permanently enlarged the brain's sugar-craving center—I'd done a blueberry trifle with crème anglaise. Enough so everybody could have seconds, with Douglas's dessert wine.

I was just leaning back in my chair (which had come with the house and was slightly unsteady), exhaling, when the visitor from Ithaca, Jay, who was seated on my right, lowered his voice and allowed as how he didn't eat anything with sugar.

"Are you diabetic?" I asked, surprised.

"Hey. That doesn't follow. Would you ask if I was an alcoholic if I'd wanted a Coke? Or if I was a second grader if I said I didn't eat library paste?"

I wasn't sure what was going on here, with this agreeable stranger next to me. Something unexpected. I glanced down the length of the table at Douglas, who was talking to Carole on his left and Winifred on his right. The moment hung there while I shifted my gears.

"Eating paste," I said. "Heavens, I'd forgotten. I used to wonder if there were actually kids in my class who did. And what is it they eat with a vitamin B deficiency—dirt?"

"So, Nan, aren't you going to offer me half a grapefruit or something? I usually manage to make my host extremely anxious when I push away dessert." He had dark eyes, and just a half smile. As if he was half kidding. He'd worn a pink shirt and royal blue tie. I suspected his bright colors were for much the same reason that I'd been wearing a lot of red.

"That's because she's usually obese," I said, "and so takes it as a judgment."

"Is that right? Does that mean you aren't?"

"Obese?"

"Going to offer me something without sugar?"

I leaned forward, studying this man. "Is this a controlling maneuver? Shall I make a large production out of carrying in a sliced banana with, ummmm, a few blueberries on the side on which I squeezed lemon juice?"

"I'd be obliged."

"No, you're wanting me to feel obliged."

He held up his coffee cup as if in salute. "I'd be obligated to you if you would."

"Already, I'm obligated to you."

We were having a good time, playing around, like new friends at recess. Had we been alone, I'd have been tempted to say, Go slice your own fucking banana, and we'd probably have been on the floor in minutes.

That was the moment when I realized that this supper party was not going to solve the trouble between Douglas and me after all.

I looked down at the orange-clad English teacher, Bethany's young mentor, and wished mightily that the woman had thrown herself at this visitor, or that he had thrown himself at her.

What was going to happen if we continued the way we were, Douglas and I, was that I would have an affair—if not with this man, then with the next who came to town, some stranger who didn't know our history, who didn't know the gaping space where a daughter had been and wasn't anymore. And Douglas would spend more and more time writing his preacher, calling, clinging to what was left of our daughter, losing touch with those of us who were still here and near.

I got up and fetched the visitor a plate of fruit and handed it to him. I watched him eat it. No more than six years younger, I figured. And, anyway, what did all of that matter if you weren't selecting a father for your child? Younger, dumber, shorter, poorer, one screw loose? You didn't have to factor in anything if you didn't plan to parent with the man.

We sat on the side of the high bed, thighs touching, the quilt on the floor. We were still in our nightclothes, watching the first morning light come through the upstairs window. The window was open, and the scent of pelting rain in the air. I turned to Douglas for a kiss; he ran his hand over my hair. We'd made love again, turning together in the night, ready, hoping the warmth of the evening and our neediness would mend us. At least apply a patch.

"It went well last night," I said.

"We give good parties," Douglas agreed.

"We do. Winifred seemed touched to be included."

"I never cared for her husband."

"Just so she did."

In the kitchen, the coffee dripping, making that morning smell which was so reassuring, I buttered my toast while he poured milk on his cereal. "Carole thought my watching a transplant might be helpful for me, she said."

Douglas looked up from slicing a banana. "I'm sorry you put her through that. She's had a hard time of it. I thought we agreed not to talk about our daughter at the party."

"She was asking about the Houston trip—" I could feel myself on the defensive.

"Yes," he said, "she's been understanding about all that." He was drinking his coffee from a blue-glazed handmade mug some grad student had given him. Thick, with a wide lip and a flat handle. Reminding himself, maybe, that he was liked, received gifts. Which mattered more to him than the fact that the cup was next to impossible to drink from. Another difference between us.

"I was thinking about—the Reverend Clayton," he said, getting up to refill the clunky cup. "How finding him was almost—how it must be a bit the same as those young adults you read of who set out in search of their real parents because of their need to know who their blood kin are. You understand, Nan? And if I wouldn't have picked, that is, wouldn't have thought to pick him out, well, as Calvin C. said, God moves in strange ways." He kept his back to me, adding skim milk, his voice difficult to hear. He was confessing belief; he was sharing this with me. That was Douglas, too, not one to evade or cover up where he stood on matters.

One time I recalled Doris and I were talking about how couples got together. She was daydreaming about their first meeting. "I wish I had a videotape," she'd said, "of what David Senior's face looked like when he first saw me. We were a blind date, fixed up by my roommate at Syracuse. He was her brother. I don't know if I fell in love with that look or if he fell in love with mine. I thought he was the greatest hunk I'd ever seen, or whatever we said in those days, dreamboat."

I'd replayed the evening Douglas and I met at the apple strudel cafe, the student hangout on Chicago's North Shore, but that wasn't really the transaction that interested me. It seemed clear enough. We'd been lonesome, glad to be away from home but glad, too, to hear the sound of it at the next table. I didn't think it was some sort of chemistry. I'd even have waved at her lump of a geographer if I'd heard that Texas accent. Feeling at the time in my escape to Northwestern that I'd renounced my birthright, when all I'd actually done was to pack up my clothes and enroll in some tough courses.

What interested me, had through the years and did now with staggering force, was how the covert marriage contract between couples got set in stone. Maybe it granted the wife the right to cry in any crisis and granted the husband the right to curse all other drivers. But then when the man wept all night or the woman yelled "fucking pig-snout" out the window at a motorist, things fell apart. The marriage became null and void.

What had Douglas and I agreed to?

That my work would stop short of a degree. That the number of children in our house would not exceed the number of parents. That we could have abundant friends in common and separate friends of the same gender. (But where did that leave a man who liked to be a teacher between the sheets as well as in the classroom? Where did that leave a woman who thought all anguish was eased by the body?)

I believed that couples could draw up lists until the cows came home about who carried out the recyclables and who got the automobiles inspected and who balanced the checkbook, easy as crackers and cheese, as Jesse would say. But that was just window dressing. The real rules were all worked out in a sign language which was never translated.

I was thinking all this about Douglas and me, and about

what happened to such rules when the marriage hit disaster. When it foundered against the jagged reefs of loss.

Douglas had been permitted the final word on human consciousness, that was his area of knowledge. He could call himself the donor of our daughter's heart. He could claim to know what was her and what was not her. Defining life belonged to him.

One day before too long, he would go to Houston to the Reverend Calvin C. Clayton's church to hear the frail man preach. A congregation of five hundred, all singing and shouting for joy, their preacher living on borrowed time with a borrowed heart, a miracle. He wouldn't be the only white there, but they would know who he was, and they would file by and shake his hand afterward, tears of gratitude pouring forth. And Douglas would tell how he felt Bethany's presence, how he felt her heart warming in its new incarnation. He would decide to make a gift to the Missionary Baptist Church in her name. He'd let them take his photo with the preacher. Next year they would stand together at the candlelight ceremony where this year the hiker had stood with the balding man who'd walked his wife's lungs to the top of Mount Elbert in the Rockies.

"I think I will go to Sanibel for a spell," I told him. "Give us both some time to think."

"You hate Florida in the heat," he said, standing at the counter as if he'd forgotten why he was there. His banana uneaten. "The tourists will be out thicker than mosquitoes."

It would be steaming, of course, Douglas was right. I fished the paper out of the recycle sack and saw that it was already in the nineties on both coasts of Florida. As if the lapping sea itself heated the shores, like hot water thawing chilled hands.

We'd lived in cold climates since we met, Douglas and I. Who would we have become instead, I wondered, if our moves had been in the other direction? Two university students from, say, Minnesota, getting their schooling at Palo Alto, marrying and raising their young in Tuscaloosa? Who would we be now?

"I'm off," Douglas said, slipping on his backpack, tucking his reading glasses into his shirt pocket. Reaching for an umbrella.

"You may need a sweater," I told him. "It's not as warm out as it looks."

I smiled, hearing myself, hearing us. Even as we ripped our life apart like a sail in a gale, we went right on with the business-minding language of the long-married. Him reminding me I didn't like Florida in the hot weather; me telling him it was cooler outside than he thought.

If all the parts of the bicycle were replaced, was it the same bicycle? Apparently so, if you still claimed it as yours, if you still had your memories of it.

❧   ⑥   ❧

I would try going away, putting most of the length of the East Coast between us. Sometimes the mind worked that way. It sensed a great distance, yet here you were, leg touching leg on the side of the bed. The signal went out that there was trouble. But if, in fact, there was the distance of twelve hundred miles between you, well, then your system made sense of the feeling of distance, of separation. We would miss each other, Douglas and I; we would shift our focus from constantly missing our girl. I would beachcomb, fossil-hunt a young coastline; Douglas would slice rat brains, write his preacher. We'd sleep alone, eat alone. And, in time, our bodies would send out a distress message: get back together.

Outside it looked like the start of a week of soggy weather, rain lashing against the house, dark skies, ankle-deep puddles, all good for the flowers and, in some inverse way, for the spirit. The sound of watering.

I packed away the last of my cold-weather clothes in my cedar closet off the hall on the second-floor landing. I bought a round-trip ticket to Fort Myers, with the help of Fern, the travel agent, unable to imagine that I would not be coming back. I arranged to rent a heap. I let Doris know what was going on, supplying her with the Sanibel Island number. I left a message on the "Alison and Bert aren't here right now . . ." machine, inviting them to show up anytime, giving directions for before and after the causeway.

I cleaned the downstairs and packed away the party feast. I moved the iris upstairs to the window seat. I paced through the children's rooms. My nose ran but I did not call it crying.

Starting to make the bed, lifting the "star-padded" quilt to fold, I came unglued. All of Bethany's childhood slips of the tongue came back, things that had got embedded in our family vocabulary. The time at Jesse's ranch she called the spice rack a "lazy bruisin'," and we had later used that to refer to R-rated movies. "Don't see it, it's a lazy bruising." The "hardwire" store where we went for cup hooks and picture hangers. "No, that's up here," Douglas had said, amused, pointing to his head. Later, sometimes calling his lab the Hardwire Store. Her helping me mail letters in the "postsophist," which gave us a good term for tedious academics: post-Sophists. How we had carefully excised those codes in the past six months.

Digging for Florida clothes in the spare room off the upstairs hall that we sometimes called the upstairs sitting room, I found a bathing suit that looked as if it had seen better years (perhaps we were the same age?), a newer black tank suit with the faint odor of chlorine still clinging to it, and, wrapped in a striped towel, a yellow T, a pair of red shorts, and a pair of new red Keds which I couldn't recall buying. Had we taken a family vacation? Last summer was a blur. From Bethany's graduation in May to her trip to Texas for Thanksgiving had been more or less wiped out of my mind.

The room was difficult enough to be in anyway. The walls were plastered with bicycle and umbrella pictures. How did things like that get started? I'd had a print taken somewhere in England that showed an umbrella hanging up to dry over a bicycle. I'd thumbtacked it to my wall at Northwestern and kept my bicycle under it. Later, I used to lean the kids' bikes under it up here, in nasty brutish weather.

Children like to have something concrete to give parents, and so, over the years, other bicycle and umbrella postcards, posters, snapshots, appeared. And then, one year, for a lark, when Bethany was in junior high, the kids sneaked in and sat up all night—it was for my birthday, forty, oh, my—and pasted snapshots of themselves on all the bikes and holding all the umbrellas. Funny, silly. A family album stuck on the wall with map pins.

Shutting my eyes, I could see her the way she looked when she came to get me and drag me in here for my birthday surprise. The fortieth was a big adult milestone, but you didn't think about kids taking note. She was in that instant of turning, at thirteen, from a hard-training, plain-faced athlete, all legs and concentration, into a gentle, rounded young woman, lit from within. It had made me wish I'd known Douglas at that same moment in time, poised on that same ledge.

And when she tied a scarf around my eyes and tugged on my hand, saying, "Come on, Mom, I'll lead the way," it made a tight feeling in my chest. My daughter, growing up. And then when I took the blindfold off to see the altered photos— two-year-old Bert pasted on a unicycle in a circus, four-year-old Bethany holding an umbrella twice her size, six-year-old Bert and eight-year-old Bethany on a tandem bike—the instant was gone. She had already moved on, leaving the child behind.

It was almost too painful to stay in the room. I'd thought about taking down all the pictures, in the fall, in the bitter winter, whenever I opened the door, forgetting, and my eyes slammed against the memories. But it hadn't seemed fair to remove all traces of my son from the house as well. . . .

Now I sat holding the red Keds (my size) and the red cotton shorts (ditto), and tried to focus on last summer. I felt as if I was in one of those films where they put the actor under hypnosis and she recalls the long-forgotten scene. Only not much came back. We were all four together on top of an outcropping of rocks, looking down toward a valley. Well, that could have been almost any side trip in upstate New York or its southern tier: the Alleghenies, Catskills, Adirondacks. Or just some nearby foothill with a view. I was sitting and so was Bert. Bethany was doing leg thrusts to work her calf muscles. Douglas? Where was Douglas? Behind us? Starting down the rocky hill? I didn't know, couldn't see. But he was there; he was speaking.

Bert had wanted to take a dive in a gorge that sounded like a death trap.

Bethany had said to me what she always did when I began to fret over him, "Don't be a Nanny Mom. They're *his* lungs."

From somewhere Douglas said, "I forget you went to public school."

But then I might not be remembering at all. Those could well be voice bites stored in my mind—the way you can sometimes hear people in dreams just as clearly as if they were speaking to you. I had certainly heard those same voices on a dozen family trips.

There was also a fossil book wrapped in the towel. I'd bent two pages (it must have been me, who else?): one was a tiny two-segmented blind trilobite called agnostid. The other, an old friend of some thirty-five years ago up the road from Round Rock, Texas, *Dikelocephalus*. I didn't know if I'd been setting out to find them or if I had. Or if it mattered at this point.

When Douglas called, I was about to ask him, Where did we go last summer? But he had on his neutral teacher's voice that stopped me in mid-thought.

"Nan? The university wants to do a memorial for Bethany."

A memorial service? But they had that. "What?" I asked him. "What do they want to do?"

He hesitated, then his voice came over the line in a modulated tone. "A memorial. Carole's in charge of it. I've asked her to come by the house, so we three can talk about it. I don't want this to be something we do up here on the hill that you don't have input into. I want this, at least, to be something we two can agree on. I want it to suit you."

Patience. I tried to grasp his words through the barrier of his patient manner. His pacifying manner, as if I was the shrew from the Blue Lagoon. But surely he was right. A matter we can agree on. We should be united on this. I rose and leaned a hand against a flat miniature umbrella, listening to the downpour outside. "Why not have Carole come for supper," I suggested. "I have food for a multitude. We can eat party leftovers."

"I'll ask her," Douglas said, cautious. "She doesn't like to intrude—"

Was this new, his speaking for her? Or was this just his team-captain way? "If we're all going to talk it over," I said. Wondering why it required a committee meeting to hang a plaque. What was the agenda here? I hated it when my husband spoke to me in his reasonable voice. Idly, I put on the red Keds. It appeared I had already been in my red mode last summer.

"Let's leave it, then, that I'll call you back if that's not fine."

"Good," I said. Wondering mildly if Carole the English teacher was sitting in Douglas's office while he talked to me, while he observed that she didn't like to intrude. Did he smile in a kind way as he said it?

I got on clean jeans, put on the discovered yellow T, moved up and down in the canvas shoes, so new they all but squeaked. I took a last look at the wall of photos in the so-called upstairs sitting room which I'd sometimes thought of making into a study but never had. Here were ten-year-old Bert and twelve-year-old Bethany, holding umbrellas that came up to their waists. Here they were as infants, glued to the handlebars of huge Schwinn bikes.

Adios, kiddos, I said to them. The lazy-bruising hard-wired post-Sophists are on their way.

Douglas and his teacher came into the house drenched, shaking like wet dogs, their umbrellas still pouring. They were laughing as they removed wet gear, accepted towels to dry their hair.

"What a wind. These things turned inside out twice," Douglas told me.

He went upstairs to change, while Carole unwrapped a thick slicker, ran her fingers through her hair, and at once seemed dry, calm, collected.

"Whew," she said. "What a day not to take the car."

I didn't mention that of course I could have come and picked them up. Instead, I poured them the best of the remaining red wine from last night and, while Douglas read the label he had himself selected, went in the kitchen and squeezed myself a glass of fresh grapefruit juice, getting pulp all over the counter, feeling suddenly in need of the citrus taste, thirsting mightily for just that taste.

For a brief instant, I was tempted to carry the dripping umbrellas upstairs to their likenesses, but resisted the urge. This was not a playful pair.

As they beat around the bush, working up to their task, it became clear to me they'd already been talking about Bethany. All the way on foot in the deluge down Stone Hollow Road, Carole from Emerson Hall, Douglas from Fenimore Cooper. Clear from the matching puckers between their eyes and the slight downturn of their lips. Carole's heavy silver earrings sliced rectangles in space adjacent to her sharp chin. Douglas had donned what could only be called a smoking jacket.

While I sat nearby on the small cocoa sofa, they took the deep chocolate armchairs from which to explain the options that, obviously, they had already discussed. Going through the motions for my sake, and that made me feel a grumpy malcontent who never knew what was going on.

"The school paper," Douglas said, "for which, as you know, Nan, Bethany wrote, wants to offer a journalism award in her name."

"English," Carole reported, her turn, "since Bethany was a major, is thinking in terms of a prize to the outstanding graduate. I don't think they intend a scholarship, but more of an honors prize. Her name would be listed in the graduation program. You were there last year, Nan, when she—at the ceremonies. You recall there were several such awards to outstanding students." She looked very earnest, and had a white pad in her lap, for notes, as if this really was a meeting.

"The athletic department—" Douglas began, glancing over at his daughter's mentor, exchanging a smile and a nod, "wants to place a jogging path around the campus pond."

"—with planting," Carole rushed ahead, eager, "that could be added to each year."

"A memorial mile," Douglas said solemnly.

"With a marker commemorating it—" Carole finished.

It took the three of us the better part of an hour and the bottle of cabernet to get around to being sure that everyone was of the same mind. And so a path it was to be. A track. The BETHANY MAYHALL MEMORIAL MILE. The curve of the trail to measure exactly a one-mile lap.

I felt light-headed on my grapefruit juice. And at once fatigued from the effort of foregone unanimity.

Our task done, Carole said, with her bright earnestness, "I told Doug he should let you watch that operation if you wanted to, Nan. He sometimes doesn't realize—" She looked over at Douglas and blushed slightly. "—I mean, he and I were so close to Bethany, we both had such strong bonds with her. But I reminded him that the mother-daughter relationship is always difficult, and that you must be having a harder time, since you're bound to feel a little ambiguous." The young woman got it all said, in her dogged, well-intentioned way.

While my husband stared at the floor.

I considered ways of enduring the crisp condescension, the cozy complicity in her tone. Was her geometric brain a rhomboid? Her tiny heart a tin triangle? Perhaps my move should be to call upon Lemonade Stand. Ask my Best Friend if she would mind taking out a teacher for me.

"I think the two of us are just more comfortable dealing with the living," Carole concluded resolutely. "I mean the miracle of the old reverend."

When the phone rang, I was halfway there on the first ring. Saying "Hello—?" in a tone that doubtless implied, *Send reinforcements quick.*

"When I hear your voice, it makes me think of your juicy fruit."

"Chewing gum?" I asked, grinning in relief, sinking against the kitchen counter, kicking a red Ked in the air.

"Not me, are you?"

I laughed out loud. God, what a tonic, laughter. What a lifeline. "Jay!"

"I knew you hadn't forgotten me. Would you believe that I set up this conference your husband is now appearing on the program of twice, just on the off chance that you would come?"

"I'll tear up my ticket to Florida."

"Better yet, I'll go get my suit."

"If you were here, there's some leftover trifle you could refuse to eat."

He laughed at that, and I thought he sounded as glad for the teasing as I was. Reality was an epidemic no matter where you lived.

"Is your lesser half around—?" he asked.

"He is." I made no move to put down the phone.

"We've had a cancellation—" He didn't sound in a hurry either. "Just the biggest name in the field, that's all. I guess you'd better fetch him."

"Sure thing."

"I'd be obliged."

I laughed again and called for Douglas.

In the living room, I sank back down on the small cocoa sofa and stretched out my legs. I was underdressed in my jeans and excavated yellow T. "That was hard," I told Carole, thinking of the memorial-mile business. "Talking about all that."

"On the phone?" Her arm looked thin above the clunky bracelet. Her shoes, out of their galoshes, had pointed toes which looked as if they must hurt her feet.

In her presence I felt, at forty-nine and counting, both as

old as Methuselah and at the same time an eleven-year-old tomboy in the presence of a high school girl with charm bracelet, locket, smooth hair, ruby lips. The very sort of female my mom had wished in vain her only daughter would molt into. "No," I said. "That was Jay on the phone. The biologist from Ithaca, that you met here last night?"

Carole brightened and turned her head, as if to glimpse the two men having their conversation. "I wanted so much to talk with him. Doug has told me all about their interesting identical-twin research, but I didn't know the first thing to ask, actually, when it came right down to it. That isn't my field, you know."

Douglas's type, clearly.

"I meant the memorial," I explained.

"No wonder that was hard for you," she said, showing her sympathy. "But I'm glad you agreed with our choice."

In the kitchen, I took off my apron and tossed it on the counter. I chewed on what was left of the grapefruit. Douglas was saying his goodbyes, giving his assurances, behind me. It took a good deal of restraint not to reach for the phone when he was about to hang up, continue my cheering conversation. I took the warmed-over ham out of the oven, both hands mitted and careful.

Douglas came up behind me and touched my shoulder. "I hope you didn't let what Carole said get to you," he whispered. "She and Bethany were pals, as you know. She's just trying to deal with it in her own way. It hasn't been easy for her."

"I know," I said in an understanding tone, setting the pan flat on the stove, not burning either of us. Thinking that if anger was the glue in a marriage, then placation was the solvent.

Why did the very event that should bind a couple together rend them apart?

4

I slept deeply and woke refreshed for the first time since the wreck, taking my early morning walk to Blind Pass just as the slanting first daylight hit the glistening jetty rocks. Such a difference ten minutes made to the light, to the tide. This morning, waders, human, bent with nets and buckets in the gray, dawn-reflecting water, while on the flats, waders, birds, stirred the shallows, rousing their breakfast.

I felt I'd come home.

The stark, dark snakebirds, anhingas, known to consume crabs and even small alligators, skewered fish, tossing them high and swallowing them whole. Nearby, the black cormorants looked heavy-throated and hungry. Pink spoonbills snapped spatulate beaks. High in the treetops, the ospreys, still in the shadows, slept off yesterday. The yellow-headed night herons hid in the tangled roots of red mangroves, dozing after a feast of fiddler crab, frog legs, turtle meat. As daytime reached the blanketed clouds above the low-tide waters, a rainbow appeared, arching from the jetty toward the wading birds. The flats became a plot of gold.

The coastline changed with every storm, the distance between the two islands, Sanibel and Captiva, growing greater or less with the tides and the squalling winds. Blind Pass sometimes just that, too narrow to navigate; sometimes a deep channel dividing the strips of land.

I was ready for breakfast, ravenous. When the day rose up behind your back and shed light on what lay before your feet, it was time to take cover and feed.

Arriving yesterday I'd felt welcomed by the place itself. When I crossed the causeway, hit the San-Cap Road, passed the Ding Darling Wildlife Preserve and the Lazy Flamingo and turned into the shell-encrusted drive, the temperature was already heading for the nineties.

Inside the snug summer cottage, I'd gotten the water and lights in working order. Pulling on faded, frayed, familiar denim shorts, still folded in the drawers under the stair landing (from how many summers ago?), I could have been that young mother again, watching amazed, as Daddy Mayhall attached a hammock to the foot and then the head of the big bed, put my new daughter in it, and, stretching out, rocked the baby to sleep and then fell asleep himself, his big, already-white head propped on two plump pillows.

The feel of the story-and-a-half weathered place was the same: a scrubbed, well-tended ship. It had all come back to me, our summers, through my feet as well as through my eyes. The wide floorboards painted white with deck paint, so many coats they were almost planks of paint. From the long main room, which opened on the front to the salt-sea air, to the screened back porch beyond which lay the inlet and the pass, it felt handed-down and safe. Wide steps in the big room led to a wide landing where my small children had slept, and narrower steps from that to the sleeping room upstairs, for guests, or for Douglas, the only son, and his wife.

The couch and bulky stuffed chairs were all covered in white duck with a faint, faded frond-filled print. The wooden dinner chairs at one end of the long room had been painted and repainted until they were glossy and smooth. The outside shutters, used to keep out the driving rains of squalling hurricanes, were white also; those inside, in the afternoon pulled shut against the slanting west-hung sun, were a deep green. A green, when Jesse was here, echoed by vases of leaves and bowls of cold apples.

It seemed to me that such a place as this, changing with the winds and tides outside, unchanging, secure inside, had a restraining quality which prevented accident and aging. Staying as it had always been, it could be navigated in the dark. Here, Bethany would not have had that wreck. Here, Douglas and I would not have got wrinkles on our thin skin. Here, I could have remained a young bride being embraced by a new family.

Field guides to birds, shells, mammals, stars, still lay scattered on rattan end tables, a couple on the floor by one of the huge stuffed chairs. I could recall Jesse and Daddy talking: That's a great white, no, that's a snowy egret. That's a great blue, no, see, that's a little blue heron. That's a skimmer, wait, it's a cormorant, the way it stands there like a stick on the dock post, no streak of red. The field guides folded and worn. Jesse and Daddy's field glasses, still on the kitchen counter by the back door, fine-tuned much stronger as the big man's eyesight had grown weaker. By the screen door, aerosol cans to repel the tiny chigger-sized no-see-ums.

I stood a bit with my after-breakfast coffee, looking out the screened door of the back porch. Here was where Daddy Mayhall had kept the telescope set up, for peering across the

placid inlet at the distant nests high in the cypress trees. I bent
to look and could see a snowy egret on a limb. Nothing had
been packed away or moved, and I realized that Jesse's "tenants" had been an invention to make it sound as if the place
had been occupied.

They used to catch sea hares in buckets and let young Bert
reach a hand in the warm water, push back the soft flaps of
the ancient creature, and find the curled shell within. The
sea hare a gastropod, which always raised the question: Had
every shell you found on the beach once been no more than a
little pack on the back of some great, soft, swimming creature? Shells seen then, not as homes, but as early attempts at
backbones? Invertebrate to vertebrate simply by growing too
large to come inside.

I adjusted the binoculars and focused on an osprey. I liked
looking into their high nests. And at the dark edge of water
under the arching arachnid legs of the mangroves. I loved the
saltwater wetlands and the waders. I loved Sanibel. Jesse used
to keep track of the tides, saying it was a female thing. Two
2.8 days this month, she'd note. She kept a tidal calendar, a
lunar calendar, a birthday book, all stacked together, as if they
were gradations of the same thing. How could Jesse not bear
to come here? Was she keeping track now of the breeding cy-
cles of her slow-chewing cattle?

I sat on the dock and removed my shoes, scooting onto a
seat in the rowboat. Never stand getting into a boat or canoe,
Daddy Mayhall's voice came booming out. They'd had more
than one guest fall into the water. Safe warm inlet where the
Caloosahatchee River slipped around the islands into the
Gulf. I raised the binoculars. Did the higher power make my
eyes as good as those of the osprey who stared back at me?
Humans had an advantage, enhancing their not very accurate
senses with all manner of aids.

The mangroves hunched, spread-legged, over the water's edge, thick as a crowd at a parade, the taller nesting trees behind them. I'd never expected to come here all alone—too many absent people, too much past filled the house and spilled even here into the outside. Perhaps that was why Jesse didn't like to come.

In the expected order of things, one day not too far down the road I'd have thought to find myself minding someone small here, cautioning her about standing in boats. Adjusting her oversized sun hat to keep off the glare. Thinking how much she looked as her mother had so many years before.

Douglas had been on the wrong track, calling me a naturalist. Naturalists focused on the big picture. They studied the ecology of Indonesia; they plotted the migrations of specific finches for a decade; they worked in statistics, in patterns of interbreeding. They didn't sit in a rowboat watching a blue heron stroll the backyard of a cottage, lifting and setting down its slender stilts, or watching a black skimmer dive for its catch. Thinking of one person who was never returning.

∽   ⑥   ∽

The phone was ringing when I got back, sweaty and thirsty. To my surprise, it was Bert. The slight resistance I'd felt answering, the hesitation of my "hello," at once vanished. I'd thought him out of pocket, over his head under water in the porous, Swiss-cheese formations of north Florida.

"What's up, Mom?" he asked.

"I'm here, at Sanibel." Well, naturally, he knew that, since he'd called the number. It was a larger answer.

"You gonna be there this weekend?"

"For some time."

"I might drive down." He aimed for a casual tone.

"How come you're not diving?" I tried to match it.

"You don't read the papers lately? Georgia and Florida are flooded. Return of the Marshlands."

"I didn't see that." When had I even seen a paper?

Bert cleared his throat. "I lost a buddy last week. Good buddy." A boy trying to sound like a man, trying to show he could talk about death as if it was commonplace. "They get light-headed, breathe too fast—the breathing mix that lasts an hour on the surface lasts about two minutes when you go down deep. You wonder what they're thinking about, guys like him who know better." His voice caught. "Maybe they're getting high, forgetting stuff."

"Bert, I'm sorry." Some mother—not me, not this time—got the terrible phone call. It hadn't been my Bert; but it was always someone's Bert.

"Yeah," he said.

"Why do you do it?" I asked, not for the first time. "Is it the thrill of pushing yourself?"

"Thrill?" His young voice rose.

"The experience—" Mothers always used the incorrect word.

"That's one side effect, okay, thrill. But a sprinter doesn't break the tape running the hundred-yard dash and then puke on the backstretch in order to puke on the backstretch."

I laughed. "Maybe they do."

My son laughed, too. "Okay, maybe they do. How the hell do I know? Maybe the race is just an excuse. Maybe those folks, like you used to be, dig up those skulls in Africa in order to get heat stroke."

"Possible." I watched something black dart across the yard. A fish crow, a year-round resident. Not wanting to take offense at his casual reference to my past work.

Whooping cranes had a route wired into their brains that took them back to the coast of Texas every year. Perhaps diving the spongy innards of Florida's submerged caves was wired into Bert's. If all information came into the mind through the body, then he'd certainly have encyclopedic knowledge by now. Maybe that's why he and his buddy (one of the unlucky ones) all but burst their lungs: to get an information fix, to send themselves a bulletin from time to time.

"We can drop lobsters in boiling water or something," Bert said.

"The market here has everything—"

"Alison'll be with me, if she can stand me out of my rubber suit."

"I'll count on it." How I ached to see my child, and how hard I tried to keep that from my voice.

"No family talk," he warned.

"No family talk," I promised.

"Thanks, Mrs. Mayhall, ma'am."

Good news that he would come. Maybe losing his friend had reminded him that I might be grateful to see him.

I walked about the cottage, glass of grapefruit juice in hand. Daddy Mayhall's personality still inhabited the place. Next to the medicine cabinet in the bathroom he'd hung a framed rubbing of a tombstone which read: I TOLD YOU I WAS SICK. And, over the telephone in the kitchen, a framed page from an old medical book his doctor had found for him when he was first diagnosed with angina:

The increase in the incidence of angina pectoris may be due to some specific deleterious influence at work during these last decades, such as the telephone with its terrorizing clang.

His humor had been abundant, and when he remarked of someone, "He's a stingy bastard," he was usually referring to laughter rather than to money.

How was it I'd married a man without that trait? Next time around, if or when, perhaps I'd place a personals ad that said FDWF seeks FDWM—F for Funny. No, I'd say FSF seeks FSM. You couldn't, after all, in today's world require them to have a divorce, maybe they were widowed or living apart, or (as was increasingly common at our age) married to an alcoholic or someone coming apart at the seams. You surely couldn't specify race. Maybe it wasn't all right to specify gender either. You couldn't specify their education. Or that their name read like a corporate merger on a solid oak door, or that they couldn't wait to get you out of your clothes, or that they liked what they found when they got there. F, you could say, seeks Funny. So how did I end up with someone as easy to cut as butter? Douglas's feelings seemed to be a mirror of his body; wherever you pressed a fingertip, he turned red.

His call, the one I'd been half expecting, half dreading, came when I was towelling dry my tangled, unruly hair.

"I tried to call earlier," Douglas said, as if this required some explanation on my part.

"Bert called, if the line was busy. Before that, I took the rowboat out." Why did I feel I had to give him the details of my morning?

"What am I supposed to tell people, Nan?"

"Tell people?" This place needed a portable phone. I perched up on the kitchen counter, my bare feet dangling.

"About why you're down there."

"That we need to think things over?" I'd had a shower and still felt damp. One forgot that the humidity on the coast was give or take a hundred percent.

He let a moment go by. "I'd just as soon not announce to all and sundry that, on top of what we've been through, they have further cause to worry about us."

"All right," I said. "United front."

"Nan—"

"All right, truly. I can see that—we've had our share of concern."

"It seems to me we have."

Tell them you have a girlfriend, I wanted to say, but caution held me back. That he would confirm it; that it would open a chasm we couldn't cross. "Carole has been helpful during this, hasn't she?" I said instead. "About the memorial?"

Again a pause, then his manly, truthful voice, "She has been a source of comfort. None of this has been easy. She seems to understand my feelings about the Reverend Clayton—"

That's because you both believe in reincarnation, I thought, but held my tongue. He liked her, the bandbox-fresh English teacher with the geometric earrings, because she didn't use the word *death*. What if Dr. Frankenstein built that big-shouldered Boris Karloff body to enclose a heart he couldn't bear to let go of?

"Nan?" Douglas said in my ear. "Are you there?"

"I was thinking."

"What do you want me to say?"

I saw that even my feet were still damp. "That I've gone to visit our son. Surely all the people who fed us and worried for us and checked on us, all the people who've been there for us, can understand that I, we, would want to see our remaining child. What's so hard to explain about that?"

Now it was his turn to hold the phone without speaking. Was he on the portable phone upstairs? In his study? Eating Grape-Nuts?

Finally, he said, "How was Bert? When you talked to him?"

He sounded winded; I decided he had climbed the stairs while we talked.

"He and Alison are coming down for the weekend," I told him. "Or whatever you say here. Coming over? To the west coast. He's keeping his head above water, because of the flooding, he says." I knew my joke would not go over with Douglas.

"His girlfriend seems quite supportive." There was a slight envy in his tone.

Christ, I thought, supportive. Female as truss. As sling. As cast. I had promised my son no family talk—but what was the Reverend Calvin C. Clayton? I wondered. That could give new meaning to the phrase *extended family*. "She has been," I said, "to all of us."

"What's that supposed to mean?" Douglas asked, picking up on my tone.

"We were never very good on the phone, were we?" I suggested. "Maybe we should move to the nineties and E-mail and fax one another." How did they deal with hurt feelings on the Internet? How did they get that exact inflection of disapproval, that subtle nuance of disappointment on-line?

He sighed. "Let's call it a day, Nan. I'm glad you got there safely. I'm glad you could get a monthly rate on a car, although I certainly don't expect you to stay gone that long." He hesitated. "If you like," he said, "if it fits your plans, I can drive your car down there after Jay's conference, and then fly back."

"Thanks," I told him, attempting to sound grateful. Not wanting to go into the ninety-two things wrong with that plan. Except to note that he had explictly *not* issued an invitation for me to come home soon or an offer for him to fly down for a visit. "We'll see," I told him. Sooner or later, we were going to have to see.

I didn't know what was going on in Douglas's head, not really. How it was for you, that's all you ever knew. Hundreds of books on Mind, including three of my husband's, and that's all they ended up with. Whether the authors occupied chairs designated Biology or Physics or Philosophy or Psychology, that's all they ever came up with. How it was for you.

"Okay, then," Douglas said into the silence.

"I'm glad you called," I told him. "Shall I phone you after Bert's been here—or do you . . . ?" I waited, looking down at my damp feet, discouraged in advance by his answer.

"I'll try," he said with effort. "I'll try to call on Sunday, if the kids will be there."

"All right." Why was it so difficult, I wondered, cradling the phone, to call his only living child? To make his fingers punch the numbers for the Sanibel cottage when his son was here? Was he afraid Bert would answer and he'd have to have a conversation? That Bert would refuse to come to the phone? Or that the deleterious effect of using the clanging instrument would squeeze his already hurting chest?

∞   ⑥   ∞

Hearing car wheels crunch the shell-encrusted drive, I pressed my palms together, closed my eyes, took a deep breath, and tried to prepare myself. It was no use; looking out I saw an image of my daughter leap out of one side of the sports car while my son climbed out the other. Calling to them both, I could feel the muscles of my neck and back tense. Giving the girl a hug, despite myself I made a half cry.

"You okay?" Alison asked, reaching out to steady me. "I guess I give you a start, don't I?"

"It's the way you move, mostly," I said. I tried to get my mind on the *wheet-wheet* of a plover, the *kruk-kruk* of the glossy green and chestnut ibis. Birdcalls at the coast.

When Bert first brought her to meet the family, his new girlfriend from Florida State, everyone had joked about it. Bulletin: Freud is alive and has been sighted at the Douglas Mayhall home on Stone Hollow Road. "Come off it," Bert had said, embarrassed. "That's okay," Alison, blond, long-legged, forthright, had told them. "My parents called Bert 'Chick' after my brother three times the first day we were home in Savannah."

"I told Bert I ought to cut my hair," she said now, waiting while he got out the bags.

"Don't you dare. It isn't, anyway, that," I said. "You girls both have—had—a good way of being in the world. Don't change that." I tried not to notice that my eyes were leaking.

"Hey, Mom."

"Hey, yourself," I said, getting a squeeze from my long-lost son.

"No family talk, Mrs. Mayhall, remember?"

"I don't even know your family, boy."

The kids had brought a sack, kept iced, of Dungeness crab claws and I cooked down some drawn butter for dipping and Alison whipped up a homemade mayonnaise for turning the crabmeat into sandwiches. Delicious. We told one another the story of how the trawlers ripped the claws from the crabs and how the Dungeness grew them back again. Imagining a great-granddaddy, a battle-scarred soldier, much decorated, recounting how many new limbs he'd grown in his lifetime.

When it was cool, the wind blowing out to sea, we sat in the backyard and watched the dusk-feeding night herons with their black caps, and the large wood storks—appearing through the field glasses as poor relations of whooping cranes, with their naked heads—settle into their nests in the sea of cypress.

Bert looked a lot like my dad, although I never mentioned this to him, Marnie Palmer the pharmacist having been only briefly in the boy's life, and overshadowed (as who wouldn't have been) by his grandfather Mayhall. But he did—same sort of country look, big hands and feet, wide forehead, ruddy complexion. Basically, my son looked like a cowboy. And the resemblance always made me feel more kindly toward the memory of my dad.

He came out, holding three drinks. "Gin and grapefruit juice," he said, making a face. "Mom, you had enough tonic for one teetotaler."

"Who is *he?*" I asked Alison, finally relaxed with her, her warm, straightforward personality having claimed the resemblance, watered it down.

"I don't know," the girl said in a stage whisper. "I thought *you* knew him."

"He somewhat resembles my son, who was lost at sea on a whaler. Of course my son, Bertram, was quite heavy. Obese, in fact."

"Dammit, I was never fat." Bert frowned, getting settled on the grass.

"Gotcha," I told him.

"Next trip," he explained, "if the rains keep up and our underwater caves are still flooded—"

I smiled. That sounded so counterintuitive: Underwater caves flooded. Yet I knew divers could get in trouble in roiling, muddy, disturbed waters. Knew, too well, all the ways thing could go wrong for divers.

"—I'm going to take a look in Little Salt Springs up the road here. It's an anoxic mix—means no oxygen—"

"I know." My son's references to my knowledge were fairly limited to archeologic digs, despite the fact that my digging had never been for anything as recent as primates or even mammals. *What you used to do, Mom,* his usual way of summing up my interests.

"—so no oxygen, no bacteria to break down the artifacts they've found there. Can you believe a giant turtle, the Galapagos kind, with a wooden stake still through it, like a spit, and you can see where it was being roasted? Naturally, they don't want anybody going in there, blowing bubbles, letting a fart even, because once you let oxygen in, the whole thing is gone."

"Sounds like science fiction, the bad guys get down to two hundred feet and open an oxygen tank."

"Mostly, they don't want scavengers trying to dive for mastodon bones and other relics to sell. Scabs."

"Where is it?"

"Up the road. Venice. It's near Venice. They've got the place fenced in, triple wire on top. Threatening signs saying your life if you step inside. I'll have to call. Get somebody from the marine science squad at Miami to set it up for me. I tried once on my own—"

Alison, who was sitting nearby, holding her knees to her chest, picked up the story. "It was like a Hitchcock movie, honestly. We unwound the chains that were supposed to be triple-locked but weren't, and pulled open the gate, thinking that there was no harm in one dive. Bert had a rebreather and some trimix with him, so he wasn't going to mess things up. But we'd gone only maybe thirty steps when about a hundred ospreys, you know how they look just like vultures, began to squawk and come flapping out of the trees, making more racket than you can believe. It scared me out of my socks."

"Yeah," Bert said. "I was still ready to go on, then I got to the next fence, which really was padlocked, and had a sign saying trespassers would be shot or something like that. Thumbscrews. The rack. And a state trooper's van was there to boot. So I said forget it, please, and we skedaddled. But I'd like to go back. It's about two hundred sixty feet deep and pretty amazing. Unique, which I guess is why all the heavy security." He kicked off his running shoes, looking terribly young to me. "Anyhow, Mom, since you're down here, I'll call them up. I don't care about the *beast bones*, but I'd like to see how the preservation works. Sulfur base, it must be."

Alison sipped her drink. "I told Bert they probably didn't even let divers with rebreathers down. They probably just sent robots."

"Would you cut it out about robots?" He raised his voice. "I'm being dumped for a robot," he said to me.

"Obese robot," Alison said.

"Robots?" I didn't know what this was about, but had relaxed with the sound of their teasing, and the gin, plus the fact that by now I was used to her Georgia voice.

"Out there in Monterey Bay in California," she told me, "they've got somebody pouring in tons of big money for this robot to look at what's in the mid-ocean. We've seen what's on the bottom, the very bottom, because you can just drop equipment down, and of course divers go down in the shallow part. But nobody really knows what's in midrange, past where human divers can go. I mean, most of life on earth is out there and we've never even seen it. Can you imagine that? Things bigger than whales, things with eight stomachs like transparent parachutes floating and eating. But if you get them in your net, a shrimp boat or something, they're just so much goo out of their depth."

The girl looked so animated in the twilight, her voice raised, her hands gesturing, totally absorbed in the facts of her story. How I could remember that thrill. That excitement at wanting to know the unknown. Alison was fortunate, just as Bethany had been, to come along at a different time, in a more encouraging world. Where whatever you wanted to do was yours for the claiming.

"I'd like to see pictures," I told her.

"There's this creature," she went on, encouraged, holding her cool glass pressed to her cheek, "that looks like a human brain except you can see through it, and somewhere inside is the real creature. And then there's a siphonophore—you know, siphons its food—about fifty feet long with all these stomachs and tentacles like glass cobwebs. You can't believe it. If some alien came, they'd say: That's the main life on earth. On top, crawling around, are these stiff little things, drones."

"I thought you liked diving. My diving," Bert said, sounding hurt. "I study breathing—how can I compete with some hunk of junk that doesn't?"

"You're a physiologist, that's different," Alison said. "You want to see how far you can go down and still come back. That's great. I'm not saying that's not great, Bert," she insisted.

"You're saying it sucks. Compared to robots."

"I can hardly stand it, it's so thrilling, to think that over ninety percent of the life on this planet hasn't ever been seen, by anybody. Come on, Mister, don't go ballistic on me."

Quarrelling? Were they really? Or was this something they were doing by instinct, the kids, exaggerating their feelings, getting my mind off my missing child, off the young man's sister, making sure that there was another agenda to this visit? If so, it was working. I would have hopped in the car with the long-legged girl at that very moment and headed out to the sunken canyon off the coast of California and never looked back.

I listened, rapt, as Alison talked about larvacean and *Apolemia*. Whole moving, eating galaxies of beings I did not know one thing about. Were there fossil remains of such things? They wouldn't turn to goo brought to the pressure of the surface, already filled in by stone. I imagined the instruments that undersea scientists had sent to the bottom to sit there like sleepy old dogs and relay what their blurry scopes could see. Not a glimpse of the mid-ocean loops of cellophane with their myriad stomachs. Mid-ocean cows, it sounded like.

But I thought perhaps they had entertained me enough, and got to my feet. "Moonlight swim?" I suggested.

Both the kids said no, they were ready to hit it. It was some helluva drive. Perhaps, I thought, they were wanting the house to themselves, the use of the big double bed while I was out of earshot. I hoped so.

Inside, I pulled on my old black tank and my canvas shoes so as not to cut my feet to shreds, and walked down the oyster-shell drive to the dirt road, and across that to the white fine sand, the salty, cresting waves now already phosphorescent in the dark. It was a pleasure being out. A few families were on the beach, you could see flashlights bouncing along lighting the path of strollers, and smell the pungent candles lit to keep away mosquitos. Smell, too, the sea and coconut oil. And crabs: someone had boiled supper.

In the water, dark and silvery, I tugged off my suit and swam out with it in my hand, sinking into the colder depths that hit my ankles, the surface still bathwater warm from the sun. Delicious, the contrast.

I let a wave take me under, throwing my head back so that my hair was out of my eyes. I did a sort of breaststroke dog-paddle into the waves. The tide was out, so quickly it was deep and all the water felt cold. I loved swimming without a suit. Douglas and I used to do this, slip off to Galveston when we visited the ranch. Take off our suits and I would ride in his lap in the water, my arms around his neck, his knees bent, bouncing with the buoyancy of the breakers. Sometimes, if it was night, we kissed and tried to make love, but it wasn't that easy, not in the salt water with the waves and the slight fear of jellyfish, stingrays, and other swimmers.

That made it almost more erotic, the attempt, my straddling him, legs around his waist. I missed the sex. Dunking myself, I shook like a dog and dived under again, letting my fanny crest the surface (no one could see), spreading my legs and fishtailing under. I could picture Douglas stripping, in our bedroom, getting to me in two strides, kissing my stomach, saying, "Baby, baby, baby." I pulled on my suit and swam back, my face under the tide-pulled waves.

By Sunday, the kids had turned a shade darker just from hanging around the beach and going out in the boat, and I had soaked up their company like a thirsty sponge. We'd seen a mangrove cuckoo with its polka-dotted tail and I'd told them it was a zygodactyl—two toes pointed one way and two the other. We'd seen a brown-spotted wader with a drooping bill which I told them was a limpkin, a large bird that gorged itself on snails.

They were kind, Alison and Bert. They allowed me to feel like their guide. It was as if my son had never been here, and of course it had been years, and as if his girlfriend from Savannah had never seen coastal swamps before. We saw a bittern straddling reeds. What else? Anything else. Passing the field glasses back and forth, drinking the tea I'd brought in a cooler—flat-bottom boats were better than canoes for that, too—wearing hats and UV sunglasses, because I told them to. We watched an osprey leave her nest and dive feetfirst into the water, looking like Icarus with her black wrist patches seeming to attach her white underwings to her white belly. The only raptor which plunges into the water feetfirst, I was allowed to tell them. Generous children.

Back in the white-painted house, the shutters closed, fans

and cold air on, we drank Gatorade and brushed the sand from our legs. We gorged on shrimp for lunch, fresh from the little market near Blind Pass, boiled and cracked while still warm, shells piled together in the center of the table. And I, at least, waited for the sound of the phone to ring, for Douglas to make his call.

Alison wore a halter and cutoffs, Bert just cutoffs. They seldom touched, treating one another like buddies, like lab partners. I understood that; all the cuddling and smooching of an earlier era, ours, had been in lieu of sex. And parity.

I wanted to talk to Douglas about that, to speak as Bert's mother to Bert's father—about their visit, their easy way with one another, the difference a generation had made. Wanted, I suppose, to show that we could still have such talk together, back and forth. That we could see some one simple scene the same way and, in comfort, remark upon it.

Just sometimes, Alison's resemblance to Bethany came back with sudden force, and then faded. When the kids were talking between themselves, arguing back and forth. The robot. "Well," she said, "they send robots down into volcanoes, don't they, and that doesn't mean no more vulcanists, does it?" Or the value of this particular cave they'd both dived, in the Woodville karst where you walked through the trees and ahead it looked just like a pitiful algae-covered pond and then it was one hundred feet tall. "Come on," Bert said, "one sixty, a huge cavern, half a mile wide." When they sat there, having done their kindly act of being good scouts on the tour, and were just themselves, rapping back and forth, I sometimes almost had to rub my eyes not to think I was seeing siblings, not to think I was back with Bethany and Bert in high school, the tone, the enjoyment of the dispute, if not the subjects, identical.

It must have been somewhat the same for the family in

Georgia, whenever the kids went to visit. For although Alison's brother Chick was alive, apparently he had just sort of moseyed out West and hadn't been heard from in more than a while. Leaving a few courses incomplete, no forwarding address. His parents must have had quite a similar solar-plexus response whenever Alison brought this ruddy, stocky, look-alike boy breezing through their house and out again.

Somewhere I had a roll of film (I had boxes of photographs, of course, that I could not bear to open), developed, of the four of them, the two sisters and their brothers, taken the first Christmas Alison and Bert were together. Taken at Mead's Mill, outside in the snow. Looking at the pictures, you could see they didn't look all that much alike, the two boys and the two girls, the features themselves. It was more, as I'd said to Alison, in the way they moved. Their body stance, their wide smiles, their open attitudes. Risky boys; stable girls.

"You making it okay?" Alison came up behind me in the white kitchen while I was washing strawberries to have for a midafternoon dessert. Thinking of the silent phone.

"Mostly," I answered. I felt small with her arm around my shoulder. I'd felt tall growing up; five six in Round Rock in the fifties, especially since none of the boys had gotten their growth at eleven. But now, shrunk by half an inch, at five five plus, in today's world I'd become a short person. I could still remember myself back then in that growing phase, with legs that jumped, ran, kicked, thrust themselves forward. I could remember the feel of that straight preteen back and the slight breasts and the new way I had to hold myself because of them. Alison must have been totally grown at that age.

"There was an item in our paper about the problems of women athletes," she said, lowering her voice and getting out bowls for the berries. "You know, bad diet, anorexia, loss of periods, bone loss from not having enough estrogen, stress fractures, and all the rest. I thought about Bethany, you know, how she was going to write about all that stuff. About the way she'd planned to cover the Olympics in Atlanta. I'm sorry about what happened to her, Nan. That isn't worth much, is it, being sorry? But—I was reading all that."

"Thanks," I said. "A lot of things remind me, too—"

"Go on in where it's nice and cool," she said. "Let me finish these. Sit down with Bert, why don't you?"

"There's ice cream—"

Feet under me on the big, soft couch, I asked my son, "Did you see about the explorer who made it to the North Pole alone, without support?"

"I don't know what you mean by *see*," Bert said, "but sure, I know about him. The Norwegian. He was a deep-sea diver."

"That's what I read."

"They used to have to climb Everest or whatever and then they had to go down deeper than anybody's been before. I guess the North Pole is about all that's left for explorers, if you want a first."

I had on white shorts and a white T. The camper's uniform for Sunday. That was probably a reflex, a hangover from central Texas camp days. I'd pulled my mop of hair up in a topknot with a rubber band. That must be from camp days, too. "What I was interested in," I said, "was that he knew how to ration his food, or rather when to speed up his intake. It said he got stomach pains when he went from eating sixty-two hundred calories to seventy-five hundred. That's not even conceivable, burning up that much."

"Yeah?" Bert half closed his eyes, as if calculating.

"I was impressed he knew how to assess the cost—of eating more food and increasing his speed rather than holding it back and taking longer." It seemed to me that my son, as a physiologist, would be intrigued by the idea of someone knowing their body that well, knowing just what he could do and what the results would be.

Bert stretched and grinned at me. "And I bet you think he was doing it for the *thrill* of getting his face frostbit and losing thirty-five pounds."

"Something like that."

"He didn't," Bert said, sitting up straight, like he was about to give me the word, his face intent. "And he wasn't doing it for the *thrill* of finding out that a person can keep his muscle tissue from being totally destroyed by consuming that many calories even if it makes him gag. He was doing it *to have done it* and to get to stand there and hoist that flag." He stood and stabbed an imaginary ski pole in the ground, thrusting his barrel chest out. "Me Norwegian."

"No," I said, getting to my feet. "No. He was doing it *to do it*." It suddenly seemed imperative that this boy understand, that he get it right. "He was doing it to have life-and-death control over one thing—making it. Everything else factored out. Don't you see? Eat your rations or eat yourself, miscalculate and freeze to death. Take a wrong turn and get trapped on a floe. You alone making all the decisions." I knew my voice was too loud, shrill, but I could feel that I was right. I knew it in the pit of my stomach.

The random drunk driver, the parents, all the crazies on the street, all the dying preachers, all the dross and trivia of living, gone. Forgotten. For that piece of time at least, everything else erased, wiped out. And then how on earth, after you'd done something like the explorer did, could you ever come back to all the silly, foolish, everyday risks like Legionnaires' disease or the new flu or the return of dandruff? Or even your own grief.

"Hey, whoa, Mrs. Mayhall, ma'am." My son sat me down. "I'll ask him, okay? When I get elected to the Explorers Club I'll ask him. Diver to diver."

"Do," I said. "See what he says." I bit the inside of my lip, wiped my eyes. Well, parents had the right to get carried away the same as anyone else. "You said yourself, about your buddy who didn't make it, that sometimes they dive to forget—everything else."

"Yeah, I did. I guess we can agree on that. Okay?"

Alison brought out dessert, and I could see she was watching me, perturbed. She'd made big bowls of berries and ice cream, somehow stirred the hard-packed store-bought brand until it seemed soft as hand-cranked. "You want some coffee or anything, Nan?"

Bert fetched us glasses of wine.

I tried to get a grip. "The explorer is writing a book," I said, "about getting to the Pole."

We talked about that, the three of us. About how the book would be an adventure story, no longer a solitary ordeal. And how it would make a great movie, because you knew the end. How in real life he might not have got there, or not done it without losing his feet or fingers. How he might have got stranded or turned back. He might not have beat out the Russian and the Japanese who were trying also.

"In the film," Bert said, licking his spoon, "the stars at night when he's setting up his tent are gonna look like the inside of a planetarium. When, the real story, he was probably half-dead and hurrying to get in out of the Arctic cold, every muscle cramping, sick enough to puke, and forty comets could be shooting overhead and he wouldn't give a rat's ass."

I took a deep breath. I hadn't realized how close to the surface my feelings were. How much effort it had taken to keep the lid on. I looked at Bert and at Alison, who were studying me, assessing me. Not a task twenty-one-year-olds should have to perform.

"Who plays the lead in the movie?" Alison asked.

Bert said, "Texas's own Tommy Lee Jones."

"As a Norwegian?"

"Harrison Ford?"

We were all laughing. "Sean Connery?" I asked.

They threw up their hands.

"Keanu Reeves?" Alison asked, and they broke up.

It was hard when it was time for them to leave. I was not going to place a call to Douglas. He knew they were here; he knew the number.

It was late afternoon when they'd packed the car and were starting the long drive back to the Tallahassee campus. You learned to be a night driver if you lived in Florida, Bert said.

"What's with Dad?" he asked, out on the crushed oyster-shell driveway.

"He's having a bad time—" What else could I say, and not be disloyal.

"You guys splitting up over this? Over Sis?"

"No family talk," I reminded him, pulling him close and kissing his ruddy cheek.

"Got me," he conceded, looking vulnerable.

"You come see us," Alison said, getting in the sports car. "When the rains quit we'll be out there in that pond under the algae. You can't miss us."

"Thanks. If I start to go mangrove cuckoo, I will."

I stood on the back porch in the sticky morning heat. I missed the kids already, and they had hardly been gone half a day. It was the pits, being lonely at my age. What was the point in investing all those years in a marriage only to stand staring at the dozing raptors in their nests, wanting company?

Yesterday I'd come unglued, carrying on about the Norwegian and his trip to the Pole. Making that scene about eating all your rations too soon or too late, which the kids had had to jolly me out of. When I was the one who should have been reassuring them, saying lean on me.

Are you guys splitting? Bert had asked. What a Today's World today's world was. I tried to imagine sitting down with my mom and dad, Mabel and Marnie Palmer, being casual or pretending to, asking, You all splitting? Over the new female pharmacist? Over whether to take your vacation at Rockport or Galveston? Over the new breadbox with the daisies on it? What an idea. They would have both passed right out in their easy chairs. Told me to go wash my mouth out with soap, to hush that kind of talk, to mind my manners. Kids today could probably ask anything. She still putting out, Dad? He still any good in bed, Mom? You guys got anybody on the side these days?

I crossed the San-Cap Road, heading for the high dunes that edged the beach, looking for traces of the Pamlico on top of Anastasia's mix of coquina, marl, sandstone. The first yellow light painted the bent backs of cotton shirts whose wearers fussed with buckets and nets. A faint tracing of rainbow curved over the jetty, then washed out in the sunlight and disappeared.

On the flats the waders had gathered for breakfast, and I searched with my field glasses under the distant red mangrove roots for sightings of rosy spoonbills but did not see any. Everything in the light of dawn looked black and white to me. Snowy egrets and pale ibis raking the shoreline with dainty feet, sleek cormorants and the snakelike anhingas drying their dark wings. Was it true they could devour a small alligator? One of these days I'd have to walk down to the Ding Darling Wildlife Preserve and refresh my memory on all the things I used to know, the things I used to show my children.

I shaded my eyes and tried to picture the first settlers, na-
tives inhabiting prehistory, subsisting on this subtropical barrier
island, feeding off the birds and perhaps alligators, too, who in
turn fed off them. The white sands the same—nothing in geo-
logic time, a bit of mist burnt off in a morning—but the coastline changed each year, with each wild tropical storm. It had
changed at least three times in my memory, the Blind Pass gap
between Sanibel and Captiva silted over, opened up, widened,
narrowed again. Not unlike two people in a marriage.

By the time I'd showered and washed my hair, I felt pulled
together enough to call Jesse, to send my very real appreciation
over the wire. "Hey," I told her, "that was a really great thing
you did, giving me the keys to the summer place here."

"Nan. I was wondering if you'd made it down there." Her
voice was a redhead's voice, firm, loud, colorful, warm as a
mesquite fire. "I hope you're on the mend."

"Still applying Band-Aids."

"Has your boy come to see you?"

"This weekend, with his girlfriend. That was a little
tough, dealing with the resemblance."

"It's a treat whenever they come."

"It is." I hesitated, not wanting to put Jesse's loyalties
on the spot. "I'd hoped Douglas would call while Bert was
here—" I was still damp from the shower, and that was cool-
ing, that and the iced breakfast coffee.

"Honey," Jesse said with feeling, "men and their losses."

I guess I was wanting some wisdom from Daddy Mayhall's
wife. She seemed to have an abundance. I remembered her
woman-to-woman advice when I was pregnant with Bethany,
her not afraid to speak right up, even though she hadn't had
babies herself. "Every man in the world wakes up with an erec-
tion every day of his life. He's dreaming of his mama. Don't
fret about it. Same way, every man has an affair when his wife

has a baby. You might say every last baby is born to a couple hovering on the brink of divorce. You've got your baby, he wants to have his. Just ask him when the time comes, how does he think it was for his dad, when his mama was preoccupied with him. That'll put an end to it." And she'd been right.

Now she said, in the same firm way, "You've just got to get some understanding around the matter. Daddy, when his older boy Walter was killed, he was an ox in a glass factory. He was a bull gone totally mad, trying to gore everything in sight. You can't even begin to imagine." She sighed. "I never saw such a sight. *Grief* is a hanky word. A bitty, church-service word. Daddy had woe and lamentation. He had your Old Testament despair. One time he literally nearly choked a man to death, a rancher from Sequin, who called him 'Walt.' The man had been calling him that for forty years and didn't know any better. I saw Daddy rise up on those big diabetic legs of his and hurl himself at that man's throat. 'Walter is *dead*,' he hollered.

"I'd forget sometimes myself," she said, "and call him that. We'd be—what do they say?—getting intimate, and I'd forget. He'd have my gown over my head, and he was a big man, and I do mean in every way, and he definitely was, and I'd cry out a little, say his name, 'Walt, wait.' And then I'd see his face turn dark, and I'd think, This is it, Jesse, girl, he's going to break your neck right here on the goosedown pillows and they're going to find him out there trying to tear some cow apart for something else to do with his rage.

"But he'd just put a hand over my mouth, gentle like—he never hurt me, I'll say that, he just put a hand over my mouth. Then his interest would go sagging down, and he'd drench the bedsheets with sweat in the night, and then he'd be okay."

I was surprised. "I didn't know that about his name—" I told her. "I thought I'd been supposed to call him Daddy Mayhall when I married Douglas, and that stuck—"

"I remember that time you got it in your head to call me Mother Mayhall." She laughed a big, loud laugh, pausing in her reminiscence.

"I remember, too. You were funny, flopped down on your back, your legs in the air."

She said, serious, "I guess it was more than that, honey, more than what I said. I guess I thought, Whoa, wait, I'm not going to drop my name just because Walt did. I mean it wasn't like I was his boy's mother."

I tried to imagine my large, volatile father-in-law going by the name of Walt. Walter Senior. Big Walter. Back when his older son was off flying those planes and Douglas was safe in school, exempted because of his studies (later, maybe, because the family had already lost one son?). I sipped my chilly coffee, a little chilled myself.

My hair was frizzing all over my head, and I found myself thinking of my baseball-cap days and the frayed old sample bag I used to carry when I was a rockhound. Back at age eleven. Being an adult was like Sisyphus, you just kept pushing that stone up the mountain and the blasted stone just kept rolling down again.

"I offered to make him a baby," Jesse was saying. "I was forty at the time, forty-one maybe, which in those days was Grandma Moses as far as having a child was concerned. Not like today, when that age is spring chicken, you see them all the time. But I offered. Walt didn't speak to me for a week. That was some bad time, let me tell you."

"At his age—" I said. I understood her gesture, but I wasn't surprised Daddy Mayhall had said no. The people who wanted to make a child the minute one died were the same people who ran out and bought a new honey-colored cocker spaniel for their kid the day Taffy was run over by a car.

"They say it's worse to lose them when they're little," Jesse said, "those tragic cancer babies in hospitals. But, honestly, I think it's worse for you when they're grown. Don't you? But listen who I'm talking to. This has got out of hand, hon. I went and picked at that old scab, not even thinking of you."

I shook my head. It was all right, whatever Jesse said. She was in the real world; she was dealing with the way things were. "I saw a funny cartoon," I told her, getting us on a lighter note. "Man in a bar complains, 'The problem with prolonging your life is that all the extra years get added to the last, when you're old.' "

She laughed. "That's it, isn't it? Anybody younger than you is too young to go."

"So," I asked, "how are the cows?"

"I'm looking into a new breed, but, the truth? All the new ones make me miss the Hereford and the Angus. I guess it's the way you wish you could still be replacing your own manual Royal typewriter ribbons and changing your own oil in the Dodge. Back when it was easy as crackers and cheese."

"I know." Jesse was saying the same thing: being a grown-up was a heap of work. "—I'm not sure how long I'll be down here," I told her. Telling her several things, probably.

"Stay however long you want," Jesse said, "but, Nan, hon, I have to say it: It doesn't help a thing, you two being apart."

"Bickering wasn't helping either—" Or maybe it was; maybe it was politeness that wasn't helping.

"Is that a sissy word for bad fights?"

"Hurting each other—"

Jesse said, "Your man isn't like my man, and you need to remember that. Mark my words, your man, if I know my Doug, is going to want to start over."

I stared at my bare feet. Sand between my toes even after the shower? How was that possible? "Thanks," I said. "For the warning."

"Women who marry into the same family have to stick together," Jesse said. "I used to think that would have been the
biggest help of all. If Walter Junior had had himself a wife."

"You want to come visit? Get a sunburn?"

"Not one little tiny bit. I'm having the time of my life.
Lady rancher busts their balls at the auction."

I boiled some pasta, calling it lunch, hot drained linguine
with a little butter and salt. For company, I turned on the
small TV set in the kitchen, which sat back on the counter and
which guests mistook for a microwave. The reception was
grainy, the electronic equivalent of an enlarged newspaper
photo. Arty television. The newscasters were giving a filler.
Telling how the British had such trouble with car theft they
resorted to any and everything: dead bolts inside the door,
a backup alarm, a padlock on the gearshift, yellow wheel
clamps. And then they got the thing stolen anyway. And in
the shadows on the set, I could make out a figure disengaging
a car from its restraints somewhat like Houdini getting out of
his chains. Loss happens, appeared to be the message, no matter how many safeguards you used to prevent it.

I couldn't get Douglas and the English teacher off my
mind. The dreadful echo of it: his early dumb affair with the
student when our daughter was born; the late dumb whatever-
was-going-on with the teacher when our daughter died. What
did this say about men, or at least about Douglas? That being
a parent was too much; that birth and death released a flood of
feeling which required the tourniquet of a stranger's arms?

I wouldn't have minded a stranger's arms myself. Someone who didn't know what I'd been going through, or me,

actually, for that matter. Some warmth against the chill. Out my window, there were no contenders. But the train of thought got me remembering the dark-eyed foreigner from Chicago, the Joseph with the white-on-white shirt and the ailing in-law.

What did I have to lose? I asked myself, dialing information. He would remember me—and we would reach out with our voices and give back an earlier, easier time. Or he wouldn't, and I could cradle the phone and take a stroll.

"This is Nan Mayhall," I said, more than slightly nervous.

"How about that?" He sounded glad to hear from me. "I was just thinking about you. That's the strangest thing. Let me—hold on, Nan." He covered the phone, I guessed, or held it against his chest.

His phone manner had not changed in a dozen years and neither had his voice. I pictured his high-rise apartment on Lake Michigan. The two of us in that king-size bed, gazing out the gray-tinted window at the gray lake, the gray sky sliding down until it became its own reflection in the gray water. A beautiful city, windy Chicago. I missed it still.

"I was dictating a bunch of garbage," Joseph said in his deep voice, back on the line. "Actually, it was a rebuttal to some prick critic who doesn't happen to think my new office building is the Taj Mahal. What does he know? He doesn't even think it's the Woolworth Building, if you can believe. 'A low-rise on a box.'" Joseph swore a bit, then calmed down. "I bet he woke up with that phrase on and just had to massage it into his prose. But how come I was thinking of you, was— Where are you anyway? Still in upstate New York? Can you hold a minute—?"

When he came back, I told him, "I'm down on Sanibel Island. Did you—?" No, I didn't want to ask if he'd heard about my daughter. I wanted to see someone who hadn't a clue what I'd been up to for the last dozen or so years, and wasn't even going to ask. "I'm here by myself," I said, which ought to have made it clear enough. "I thought I'd check on your mother-in-law's health."

"She died—" Joseph said, his voice suddenly flat and mournful. "In February."

"You don't mean it?" I couldn't help but be amused. Picturing this tough old turkey-gobbler of a crone, hollering for help year after year, her dutiful daughter coming running every time. "Truly? We could have met—sometime."

"My wife," he said, his voice now sounding wet enough to wring out. "It was totally unexpected."

His wife? Jesus. His *wife*. I didn't know what to say. How dreadful. "I'm sorry," I said.

"I told her about you," Joseph added, his tone solemn. "I was glad I had. At the last I didn't have that on my conscience."

"I didn't know—" Why was he telling me about telling her about us? Was this his way of asking me, now, if I had ever told my husband about him? Wanting to go on record, as time ran out, for that one passionate lapse?

"There's nothing you can do," he said into the silence, taking it maybe for contrition. "But thanks for calling. I was thinking about you, just this morning as a matter of fact. I thought you ought to know, but," he hesitated, "I wasn't sure if I should call or not."

"I'm sorry," I said again.

Off the phone, sitting on the floor, legs straight out, back propped against the counter, coffee spilled in two places, I couldn't decide whether to laugh or cry.

The worst, the very worst, which I would never had admitted to anyone, hardly even to myself, was that it flashed across my mind to ask: Who got her heart? What about her kidneys? Did you scatter her across Cook County? God. What a mess all this made of what should be a decent natural response of one person to another.

I pulled on my black tank suit and took the creaky rowboat out. In the middle of the inlet, I lowered myself over the edge (careful not to stand up, Daddy Mayhall, please observe) and hung there by my fingertips, dangling in the bathtub-warm water, peering into the root canals of the mangroves, looking for bodies. Black skimmers dove for their lunch. Ospreys, looking like vultures who'd lost their footholds, jumped in feet first and jumped back out, getting fish dinners.

"Who invited you?" I imagined them saying as I sank until only my nose was above the water.

"Your man isn't like my man," Jesse had said. "Your man, if I know my Doug, is going to want to start over." What a dunce I'd been. What was the major point about the English teacher? Not that she'd been Bethany's mentor, not that only, but that she was young enough to make a substitute baby. A Bethany's-teacher and Bethany's-daddy surrogate baby. With a tiny little beating heart of her own.

I began to wail. This was for the birds, I finally decided, forgetting it was not a breeze to get back into a rowboat. I'd been thinking canoe in my mind. *Thunk*—it rocked back, deciding not to take my front teeth with it. But after three tries I got my belly over the edge of the boat and my weight plopped me in. I put on a sun hat of unknown origin and rowed my smelly self home. No fish for supper. Having been in their soup, I felt like the day's catch myself.

Giving in to fatigue of the highest order, I stretched out on the big bed. Putting a white pillow under my feet, one under my head, I could still feel a rocking motion from holding on to the side of the boat and letting my body go with the flow.

Jesse had hung an art poster of a white polar bear on the facing wall. Some arctic-print show. It could have been at the

North Pole after the Norwegian left. "What's the big deal about the explorer?" the bear—there alone and with no support system—might have asked.

Under the bear, it said

Polar Bear
Ours Blanc
Eis Bär
Orso Polare

The bear looked big and kindly and white-haired and a bit scary, staring into the camera, showing his best side. I'd always thought he bore a likeness to Daddy Mayhall. I threw an arm across my eyes.

"That man's mind is as far from me as the moon plus China," my mom used to say about Marnie. I thought about Walter, Walt Senior. How he used to hook up the hammock over the bed and rock my babies, first Bethany, then Bert, until they fell asleep, then fall off himself into a snoring slumber which never woke them. Orso Polare.

Impossible to imagine Daddy charging around, tearing into everybody and everything. But then, I'd met him after the fact. A man with a saving sense of humor, a good tongue which kept him from seeming a typical ham-handed, sunburnt rancher with a new Lincoln Continental every year. In other words—I sat up straight—in other words—I threw a pillow across the room—in other words, *he lost a child and got over it*. I wished I knew how to shout it in five languages: *Eis Bär nein berserk*.

What if Daddy had let Jesse make a replacement baby?

Then right now some boy, daddyless for a dozen years, only five years older than Bert, would be knocking around, grumbling, I was the one they got when they lost the other one.

Griping, I never did squat right in the old man's eyes. They wanted me to sit at this dumbshit table and read this humongous red book I could hardly lift. A doorstop. They wanted me to read a fucking doorstop. Me, I wanted to be out roping cow ponies, but the old coot was scared every time I went to take a pee. Talk about fenced-in. Me and the livestock. At least the cattle get to go off to market. Once, anyhow. He'd be sitting around carving his initials into the kitchen table, muttering that at least he was carving up the table instead of his folks.

Douglas answered before the machine picked up. His voice neutral, guarded, said, "Hello?"

I yelled in his ear, "IF YOU MAKE A BABY, I SWEAR I'LL COME UP THERE AND TEAR YOUR ARMS LOOSE FROM YOUR BODY AND BEAT YOU SENSELESS WITH THEM. DO YOU HEAR ME?"

The line went dead.

5

I made a trip back, for damage control. Using my best
friend Doris's emergency call as an excuse.

Douglas and I were fairly formal on the phone. "Shall I
take the school van from the airport?" I'd inquired.

A pause, then, "Give me your flight number. I'll pick
you up."

So here we were, the Mayhalls, back in the kitchen on
Stone Hollow Road. Him having his cereal, Grape-Nuts it
was today, with skim milk and sliced banana. Me having my
Pepperidge Farm skinny toast, two slices, buttered. Maybe our
way of eating grain was an irreconcilable difference.

Our kitchen, mine, was one of those huge old Victorian
rooms which once must have had high chairs, cribs, nan-
nies, cooks, and a heavily bosomed and aproned wife bustling
about, being in charge. Now it had a butcher-block island work
space, and a table and four waxed and sanded chairs by the

window which looked out on the cracked sidewalk that led to the school in one direction and Chapel Corners in the other.

Outside, the runners of spring had been replaced by the wheels of summer. As Douglas and I sat, in a far too strained silence, I listened to the *thud, thud* of skateboards through the open window and watched the blur of Rollerblades whizzing by. I watched mothers pushing strollers and buggies, struggling preschoolers on trikes, and students with backpacks, hair flying, bent over the handlebars of their racing bikes. It was a Roller Derby all over town. I would not have been surprised to see Jesse's old animals going by, their legs now wheels, in the manner of toddler's pull toys: old Pettigrew, the orange tom, Hildegarde, the cowherding German Shepherd, the munching goats and ponies.

In reflex, I patted my chest, as if the old skate key on its length of twine was going to be hanging there. I could actually feel again on my feet the metal clamps tightening around my toe joints through the lace-up shoes you had to wear for metal skates. Could feel again the friction of the grindstone-like skate wheels hitting Round Rock's concrete walks. Ancient days. What had happened to all the skate keys of the past? What cracks had they fallen into, along with diary keys and locket keys?

"You didn't call," I said, "last Sunday. When Bert was there."

"My son didn't call me; he hasn't called me. I won't put you on the spot by inquiring whether he asked you about me." Douglas's voice indicated hurt feelings.

"He did," I said. What's with Dad? That's inquiring, I assured myself. You two splitting over this? That's inquiring.

I looked at Douglas, realizing it was hard to see the signs of aging on someone you lived with all the time. Even in the weeks away, I could see lines, cracks, in the Grecian vase of his face, on the fair weathered skin of his cheeks, on his forehead, around his mouth. Blonds had trouble with the wrinkles of time. Life etched them with a heavy hand. (Yet his hair seemed less washed-out, less drab. Could he be coloring it?)

I studied the sag of his shoulders, the heavy weight of the cereal spoon in his hand, the effort it took to wipe his mouth. In truth, as Jesse said, he was a different man from his father. Here was no ox in a glass factory. Here was a bystander who had been gored. Daddy Mayhall may have raged; his younger son had been ravaged. That must be how things got handed down: you became the other side of the reversible coat of kinship.

"I don't know how you knew," he said at last, coughing to clear his throat.

"What?"

"That Carole thought she was pregnant. It was uncanny, getting your call." Also unpleasant, unprofitable, and unlike me, too, but he had already said those things on the drive back from the Syracuse airport.

Now I replayed his words. Carole *thought?* Didn't they still kill rabbits? No, the animal rights people ... Didn't they kill litmus paper at least? But that wasn't the point; the point was that apparently she wasn't pregnant, the eager English teacher. My midsection went weak with relief. I actually bent over, as if the part of my spine which had been acting like a broom handle to hold me upright had been removed. It did seem possible that Douglas could have told me this last night on that long car trip, but then, in fairness, he'd have had to say they'd thought she was, and that would have made a quarrel.

Had I really believed he was trying? Had I truly dealt with the reality of his consenting to start all over with a new child? And had he kissed Carole's stomach and murmured, "Baby, baby, baby," into her soft dark bedroom? The whisper louder than thunder. For a moment, it seemed I might faint right there in the old-fashioned kitchen.

"And now—?" I inquired.

"Now?"

We had not made love last night; it had seemed awkward after the time apart, the bad feelings. And that was strange, to lie with a husband of decades and not know how to approach him or even whether such an approach would be welcome. It reminded me of nights late in my pregnancies, when I would stare toward the window, trying to get comfortable, wondering if Douglas had his back to me out of consideration for my condition, as big, gravid bellies were referred to, or if he found such a mound of double heartbeats unappealing. Offering, usually, finally, "Can I do something for you?" The alternatives to intercourse every woman knows. As if she, filled with a surfeit of hormones, was not greedy, indiscriminate, ready at all hours.

"Yes, now," I said.

Douglas studied his bowl. "We each had a different response to our loss," he said. "Why don't we leave it at that?"

"And what was mine—?" I was not cut out to live with a reasonable, measured man. My ire was rising. We were talking about him starting a new family, shedding his old one like a locust sheds its skin, adding to disaster an auxiliary disaster. If he'd been shouting, if he'd thrown his cereal bowl toward the pantry and the mudroom. If—I might have had some hope.

"Your response was to leave, Nan. To leave our house and what we have made of it."

Cart, horse. Chicken, egg. What was the point which of us acted first? He was right. I had fled to the past. He, to some roseate future.

"I was thinking earlier in the week," he said, placing his

spoon with care on the table, "that seeing Chicago again might not be a bad idea."

"We'd find it changed," I said, speaking for myself.

He nodded, turned the spoon over in his hand. "And ourselves, too, I suppose."

But I heard the gesture he was making: to pick up some part of that Nan and Douglas from the old days. And I knew it had cost him something. I was stirred to reply, but what could I say? It was true we'd find ourselves not the people we'd been then. The young Douglas in grad school imagining himself down the road, a chaired professor at an Ivy League school, with six kids following in his footsteps. While the young Nan was picturing herself picks in hand, digging, digging somewhere, Dr. Palmer-Mayhall, leading her team into the burial grounds of a young planet.

"Maybe we haven't changed," I finally said, "maybe the world has."

He rose, with that look on his face that said he was ready to head off for the campus. "Now? I don't know that I can answer that, Nan."

I rose, too. "Do you remember the vacation we took last summer?" I asked.

"Why?" He seemed wary. "I need to get going."

"It's been nagging at me, that I can't remember."

"I'm sure I took a roll of film—" His voice sounded as if it was coming from the bottom of a well.

"I don't want that, photos." I could see he thought me asking the impossible: that we sit and look at the Last Family Summer Vacation together. Poor Douglas, how much he was willing to shoulder that he wasn't being asked to. "It's disconcerting, a blank—I just wondered, that's all. Where we went?"

He looked at his watch. "Why don't we sit out on the steps a minute, then, so we can get a little fresh air?"

We sat together, waiting a spell until the sound of skateboards, students on bikes, dogs barking behind them, finally faded from our attention.

"We took the scenic route from Utica, remember?" Douglas began. "We drove up and had a night at Old Forge and a day to look around. Then we drove on, into the Adirondacks." He sounded as if he were giving a police account of his whereabouts on the night of a crime—slow, definite, cautious. "At Blue Mountain Lake, we went north again. We had a day hike. Then, at Tupper Lake, if I recall right, we had to make a choice. Circle back west, go through Watertown, see Lake Ontario, or go east and up toward Champlain. As I recall, you wanted to do a little fossil-hunting and Bert"— he faltered slightly—"went with you. Bethany"—saying the name was costly for him—"and I went mushroom scouting. That's about it."

He was visualizing the map. He did that, carried a map in his head. It seemed to me it was a way of not seeing where you really were. Private school students did that; the map was the territory for private school students. But I needed to remember through my feet, through my eyes. The territory was the territory for me.

Something had happened on that trip that had got it knocked right out of my memory. What had I wished him to say that would bring it back for me? You got a pebble in your hiking shoes? Bert wanted to take a piss off the one small peak we got to the top of? I got grit under my contact lenses and you had to lead me down the trail? Our daughter wanted to be running and we were slowly climbing instead? But any of those things might have happened any summer, on any trip.

"Thanks," I said. "It doesn't really matter." I watched the Roller Derby wheel by.

"Would you like to go to Jay's conference with me, since you're up here? It's next week, if you recall."

I reached out from my perch on the steps and placed a palm on his knee. The offer had cost him something. The risk of my saying no, of my getting upset that his mind had been on next week, not last June. The risk of my asking if Carole would be going, too. But that was my husband, not one to shirk trouble. "I'd like to," I said. "I like those skinny lakes, those glacial fingers. Thanks."

For a moment, my hand still on him, I thought he might cover it with his own or turn to kiss me, or even, going back to our painful talk, bury his face in his hands. Instead, he strolled off toward the campus, whistling. Strange, Douglas whistling. He'd got us through some dark cave apparently. What was it? Saying that his girlfriend was almost preggers? Taking himself back to the old mountain range of a previous year? That I had not asked him about his Texas preacher? What?

I listened to see if I could catch the tune, but Rollerbladers were doing figure eights in the middle of the street, and a car horn blared.

I realized Doris had not had her surgery (breast mashed, explored, biopsied) here at the local hospital, a bulky half block wide, behind Creation Baptist and the Congregational Church. But my feet started in that direction out of habit. We had all, the friends in Lemonade Stand, made so many trips to see each other in that hospital years ago, all of us having babies. You put on a dress and took your sterling silver baby rattle or your satin-covered music box and did up your face, and were so happy that you were arriving with thin ankles and a waistline—happy for your friend, too, that she was soon to be rid of fat ankles, an aching back, and a puffy face.

Baby visits had been occasions for great celebrations. For sex jokes, for astonishment that small-chested friends now looked like Marilyn Monroe, for endless discourse on how this baby had behaved in labor, what precisely had changed this time and what hadn't, what was still elastic and what wasn't, what was stretched past hope and what wasn't—all that information women shared and traded and passed on, codes that each cracked each time, then cracked again.

As I turned, walking the other way past Elderly Baptist and up behind the university on the hill toward Angel Rock Ridge, I conceded that I'd probably started out the wrong way because I had making babies on my mind. One reason we had all made it through those years, we friends, was that we were all in it together, we were all going through that stage of having children, of worrying about how not to have them, what to name them, what their daddies were going to do while we were busy having them, at the same time. Older women, like Winifred, who looked after us, remembered that era, gave us support when it was our due, but had gone on somewhere else, to another stage, together.

What was it like for some man like Douglas who'd been a young daddy with the rest of them, becoming an old daddy? A second-time-around daddy, passing out his photos at conferences: This is my new litter. What was it like for their younger wives who had come to mothering later, after careers? Did they have a network of others in their boat? What of the come-lately children? Did they grow up at the center of a successful world, teething on opportunity? Or did they bury their parents at a young age, old before their time?

Apart from how dumb, stupid, shortsighted, self-deluding,

and generally not great his need to have a new child seemed to me, just to pick a few responses at random, the real point was not us but her. That child. Whose name was not Bethany, whose future as well as history would have been written by someone who came before.

Douglas, how could you?

Doris looked beautiful, propped up in a lavender bed jacket (an item from her maternity days, long packed away in those boxes along with skate keys and sanitary belts), all lacy and bow-tied, as if she was nursing. She had a lavender hair ribbon in her recently lightened hair, and the room was filled with flowers, dozens of pots and vases on the window seats and dressers, on the floor, on a cart in the corner. It must be that every single member of Lemonade Stand had called on Fern the Florist's florist, Fred, to do his best. He must have flown in half the flowers of Hawaii—at least of New Jersey, the Garden State.

When she'd called me in Sanibel, it had been a surprise.

"This is Doris," she said.

"I'll be right there," I told her, Lemonade Stand's ritual response.

"I wish," she said. "But, just kidding about that, I was needing a little moral support. One of my bosoms is on a growth kick."

Gradually, she filled me in on the forthcoming trip to Boston, date already set, the need for a biopsy. That the once gaunt, now porky David (whom Doris had taken to calling Goliath in recent years) had got a bad case of Geographers' syndrome from years of sitting on his duff studying maps, and his blood pressure was aiming skyward, and she was worried about him. How he would handle her trouble, plus the one kid still at home. Plus the other three, who would insist on hovering. "They're all coming back," she said. "Just for a couple of days, I hope. They all have lives, thank Artemis for that."

"Maybe that's just what I need, a crisis," I considered. Wondering if the airlines had sick-friend tickets, cousins-of-bereavement tickets. Wondering whether it was a good idea or a bad idea to go home. "I need to see Douglas," I finally decided.

"I don't want to ask how you two are getting along."

"Don't. How's Miss Sunshine?"

"She's doing great. She's joined a Codependency Mutual Aid Support Group."

I laughed at that. Where did Doris get her good attitude? Not from the people around her, for sure. It seemed to bubble up from inside like a spring. Artesian temperament. "I'll be there," I said. "This will give me an event-caused, time-limited excuse."

"I knew you'd think of something," she said, sounding relieved. "Thanks. No kidding. A million."

"Good news?" I asked her now, taking the overstuffed chair with matching lilac footstool. I'd brought her six grape Popsicles in a Styrofoam cooler.

"I hear. But did you ever know them to say, 'Gee, we didn't get a dab of it, sorry'?" Doris was beaming as she spread a towel across her silk-covered chest and began to lick the icy grape flavoring.

"Come to think of it, no." I'd put on a dress, out of reflex, thinking hospital, a flowered spring dress with full sleeves. "Still, what a relief."

"I feel like a dunce making you come up here. They're all doing their thing. Goliath—I guess you passed him on your way up—is down there with an ice pack on his forehead for the stress. And the younger girls are making macaroni and cheese to go with the pastrami they got at the market. David Junior, well, boys—is just embarrassed by me."

"I stopped at the bakery and got a blueberry pie."

"It'll be gone by the time you go back downstairs."

"What did you hear from Miss Sunshine?" Her sister being Doris's only living family member, except for her children.

"She asked me, when I told her I'd had it done in Boston, 'Why didn't you go to Rochester, that's closer and it's famous.' I said, 'That's in Minnesota.' She said, 'I said *Rochester*,' screaming by this time. 'That's *Minnesota*,' I screamed back, nearly ripping the stitches in my tit. Honestly, how she can get under my skin every time in eleven seconds flat—" Doris shook her head. " 'That's a non-secular,' she said, sounding very prissy and sure of herself. 'You're right,' I told her, 'you are absolutely right.' "

Why didn't I tell Doris what was going on at my house, with Douglas and his teacher? Because today was her day; and because I didn't need her to have to give an outpouring of good intentions and bad advice. I needed her to be there, in all her good-hearted bulk. And she was.

"Guess what happened to me?" She scooted, with effort, until she was sitting tall.

"Else? You were running out of events?" I smiled, knowing from her tone, her glow, that it was good news.

"Else." She clearly had a fine surprise.

"What?" I asked. "Paper Route made a million on the stock exchange?"

"If we had," Doris said, suddenly looking apologetic, "I'd have sent you a plane ticket so you didn't have to buy one."

"So tell. The surgeon in Boston? The operation was a front? So to speak." I was letting her delay the punch line.

She threw her arms in the air, winced. "Nan, they've asked me to be the head of Lemonade Stand. Can you believe it?"

"Doris!" How great it was when the good guys won! "Is Winifred okay?" I didn't know if I'd missed something.

"She's fine, but she said that at seventy-five she thought she ought to step down. She said she was going to do elder-hostelling and a bunch of stuff she'd been unable to do as a faculty wife. Sail to the Galapagos Islands. She's got a million plans."

"I'm so proud of you." I gave her cheek a gingerly peck, careful not to jar the bed. I looked around at all the arrangements of lilies and iris and gladioli and pink and red and yellow roses, Fred's entire stock plus more. No wonder the room looked like a botanical garden.

"I was dying to tell you face to face. I would have written you, I suppose, down there in Florida, but when you said you were going to come back, you know—"

"My. Oh, my. It's the passing of an age. Now *we're* the old guard. Remember how nervous we were at first, when we were the babyless pledges?" Which seemed, at rough count, about twenty zillion light-years ago. That meeting, after we'd already been introduced, in the OB's office. Before this part of our lives began. Me, Nan, coming from Northwestern ABD, all but dissertation. Doris, wild with love for her roommate's brother, now her hubby, leaving her degree at Syracuse unfinished.

"I'll never forget how you saved my life," she said, sniffling a little—with joy, with pride, for all those years.

"And you mine when I had my fling—" I recalled.

"I still feed big David all that spicy food."

We retold the familiar stories, until I could see that she'd grown tired, was perhaps hurting. "When is your investiture?" I asked. "Your coronation?"

"I don't know. The fall I guess. Are you going to stick around?"

"Stay tuned."

"I hope everything—"

"I promise I'll carry your ermine-lined train, whenever it is."

Doris hugged herself, carefully. "I can hardly believe it. Me, tubby old Doris, the new head!"

On the way home, leaving Angel Rock Ridge, I decided to curve down through the campus. I was not really in a hurry to get home and deal with being back in that tenured domicile, as I'd often called it, as if the tenure was to the house and town, and who could argue that?

The day was bright, the alpine sun feeling much closer than in winter: a slight turning of the earth, and the mountain meadows bloomed and grew green. The sidewalk curved quickly, and I tripped, clumsy in my dress-up shoes, a wrench, nothing to worry about. Not like those yearly ice injuries that abounded in the Allegheny foothills, not like in the bitter months where four or more people you knew were in casts or on crutches, at the least wearing those padded Velcroed support splints. I sat rubbing the bone, turning the joint this way and that, my shoes off, my skirt hiked up, and something stirred in me—the way the sun came from the right, the feel of the granite outcropping where students sat to sunbathe on days like this, the vast vista of once-English countryside below—and I looked about to see where the last quarter of a century had gone.

I closed my eyes, against the brightness of the sun, against my anger at my husband, then opened them again. Gazing at the campfire circle of steeples in Mead's Mill below.

What was I going to do?

❧　　ⓖ　　❧

Douglas and I had always done well in the car. Part of it was that we didn't have to look at one another; both of us could look ahead. In addition, not talking was companionable as we headed up the map and down the sloping hills to the Finger Lakes region and Ithaca on a clear sunny morning. He guided us along the winding, descending two-lane state road while I studied the stolid barns weathered dark as farmland, and watched the fat black and white dairy cows beginning their summer-long meal, and the turning weathervanes on the spired country churches. Thinking that if the South was the Bible Belt, then upstate New York was surely the Bible Bonnet, its churches everywhere capping its worn land and history.

The car armistice was a tacit agreement between us, one of the many in any marriage. The talk could edge close to the bone and not cut, as if real time had been suspended. An example: how much worse we would have fared after the donor-recipient party if we had not had that drive through the brush country to Jesse Mayhall's ranch.

"Don't be too hard on Carole," Douglas said to me, when we were down out of the hills, driving through fertile farm-land curved like the bottom of a shallow sea. "It was me who wanted that baby."

"Yes," I told him. "I know."

"You don't know." He kept his tone matter-of-fact. "I'm not sure myself if I could tell you, but I'd like to try it, Nan. Maybe later, when we're in a better place." He took his eyes off the two-lane and looked at me.

"All right, I don't know." Don't know why you wanted a baby? How bad you wanted a baby? What is it I don't know? The first thing about you? I could have done a vast monograph on the unclear referents in the conversation of the long-married.

"What I'm getting at, is that a lot of wishes and feelings lay buried in a person, then something like this tragedy comes along and uncovers them. It takes a while to cover them over again." He sighed.

"Yes." I knew all about the paleontology of grief. "And maybe you don't want to cover them again."

"That possibility has to be taken into account. I would guess it's a trade-off."

"With marriage?"

"With getting on with things."

He *was* coloring his hair; I could see it in the bright side-lighting sunshine. What was he thinking? If he went back twenty-five years, if he looked twenty-five years younger and had a wife many years younger than he, would that make the daughter, gone at twenty-two, simply never have existed?

I was silent so long that at last Douglas asked, "Where are you?"

"Thinking about that."

"Specifically, what?"

Specifically? Where he was, where the three of us were. "Your wanting a baby," I said. One bad nagging thought that had come to me from time to time, to be slapped away like a gnat, was that Carole's attention and kindnesses to Bethany had been Douglas-inspired all along. But that idea was too painful to endure, that my vital athletic daughter had been used. I couldn't stand to consider it. Surely the young woman had been a caring coach in the field of letters and had simply transferred her affection from the deceased girl to her next of kin, who bore such a strong family resemblance to her. I had to believe that; I had to.

"What I'm trying to say"—Douglas's tone with me was patient, dogged—"is that I am not over that yet."

What I'm trying to say, I thought, is if you have a child now—who will certainly grow up with a sign six feet high on her forehead saying REPLACEMENT—I'll run you over with your own car and back up and run over you again. "I hear that," I told him.

I'd packed a thermos, and decided now was the time to pour us coffee. This was a time-consuming ritual, the matter of not spilling it, scalding hot, on his hand or my legs, the careful passing of the mug from home, the lidding again of the heat-tight container. Drinking mine with skim milk, café au lait without the foam, because Douglas took his that way. The compromise of coupling.

"At least," he said, "this has given us both time to think it over."

Us? Douglas and Nan? Douglas and Carole? It? Having the baby? Staying married? Going to Ithaca to the conference? "What do you mean, Douglas?" I finally asked. "The two of you, to think over having a baby?" It was difficult, it was pulling teeth, to extract the correct context of each remark, delivered to the windshield. But to let them pass was to miss this chance for confidences.

"I meant an opportunity for you and me to consider what that might mean—" Douglas halted, turned to look at me again, clearly realizing it still hadn't quite been said. "—might mean that I can't shake loose from wanting another child."

"All right." There, it was said, it was out there. Now it was my turn. Now it was my place to say, If the baby's the thing, we can cut out the middle person and use me. But of course I couldn't say that, wouldn't say that. Because I thought it immoral to have a child for therapeutic purposes of one's own, something that ranged from being selfish to being a sin. But what, Douglas might argue back, if the baby were already born, carelessly left in a basket on the doorstep of the world. There already and as likely as not adopted by nuts wanting to play house or by fruitcakes trying to make like their sane neighbors in the lawn-tended homes with the satellite dishes on top. Adopt?

"Nan?"

"I can't," I said. "Don't ask it." That was unclear, too, my answer. It meant having one whatever way, meant raising any baby, even my son's half-sister. Meaning starting over. I can't do that, I confessed. Can't start all over, open myself up, give all those years a second time. I'd be a hemophiliac within the first twenty-four hours.

"I wasn't asking you to be a party to it. I know you better than that," Douglas said, speaking clearly, slowly. "I was simply asking you to hear me. I need for you to hear where I am. Not to fly off, as you tend to do, sometimes literally—as your trip to Sanibel Island illustrates—but to sit there and hear me out." He looked this time the other way, out the driver's window toward the fields.

Roadside restaurants and the outskirts of small hamlets were beginning to appear. The area was studded with historic homes you could pay money and tour to see the furnishings of bygone eras. Homes that would pass for British manor houses today.

"I'm trying," I said. I bit my lip. It was too hard to talk about these things. It was too hard to keep on about it. The Reverend Clayton's flock increasing twofold, that was one way to keep on about it. A baby was adding a dozen other ways. It wasn't that I wanted to cut my losses, I wasn't that numb, that much in denial, but that I wanted to bury my dead. Was that unreasonable? To admit that what had happened had happened. "I am goddamn trying," I said, holding back tears of frustration.

"I'm trying also," Douglas said. "Remember that."

Parking and locking the car on the main drag of the university, we left the old conversation behind as best we could. Ithaca had always impressed me—with its upright, tight houses, snug neighborhoods, swept streets, abundance of shopkeepers—as a town trying to be a city. To set itself off from the yeomen on the farms and be a bustling city of burghers. And, amusingly, as if in recognition, there was a campus cafe near the main bookstore called the Burgher King.

It seemed a good place to stop for lunch.

As we ate our thick student sandwiches (Swiss cheese, smoked turkey, bacon, avocado, and tomato on toasted rye), enough for two meals, I pondered the matter of Jay. How much of the fact that I'd come along on this trip had to do with the prospect of seeing him again.

"He's got you on the program twice, you said." I brought up the subject. "Isn't that what he told you, on the phone? Jay?"

Douglas looked gratified I'd remembered. He'd worn a light, almost denim-blue soft cotton jacket, the kind which said, I'm wearing this for the program but don't take it seriously, and a light blue and yellow plaid preppie tie, and pale yellow oxford cloth shirt. Jeans. Just exactly right for a summertime show, being up front, maybe taking off the jacket and rolling up his sleeves when he was working the slide projector. He seemed to come by this touch of class instinctively. He didn't have Daddy Mayhall's big rancher's hands, but rather had long-boned slender scientist's hands, the sort you could just picture slipping slivers of rat brain, exactly centered, onto the slide. Maybe that had determined his choice of work. Anatomy is destiny.

Douglas had several talks he'd developed—with variations, depending on the research of the decade—as he'd moved from biologist to neuroscientist to brain scientist. And each was framed in some elegant phrase, each presenting an elegant overriding truth. *Biology Is the Science of Exception. Neurobiology Is the Science of Recognition. The World Is an Unlabelled Place. Embodiment Imposes Ineluctable Limits.* The last, a sentence he'd had mounted on his wall since graduate days, was one he'd taken from a lecture by his mentor at Chicago.

Sometimes he talked about what he was doing currently on the research begun in his dissertation showing the parallel development and performance of the immune system and the memory system.

My husband was a real scholar and had earned his considerable reputation. I did not begrudge it.

"I *am* on the program twice," Douglas admitted, pleased. "But it isn't the way it sounds. Jay had me on a panel to begin with and now I'm also giving a paper. They had a rather big name, but then you—" He smiled slightly to show he remembered that this was his wife he was talking to, and that of course I knew all the players. He discussed the prominent man with me, and why he'd had to cancel at the last minute.

"That's an honor, to replace him," I said. Most of the big names at these affairs, in his field, were still male. Although increasingly there were young women at such meetings, too. Tough, able. Lucky.

"I'm also who Jay could get at the eleventh hour—" Douglas tried for a modest shrug.

"You know better than that," I said.

He nodded. He did know better than that; in fact, I was quite certain, he thought his work far better than the older man's anyway.

He relaxed a little and told me about his talk. He was going to present a new slant on his "Biology Is the Science of Exception." It was hard for me to keep my mouth shut. Here he was proving the so-many millions of possible combinations of connections the brain could make and the number of times it made such combinations daily. Explaining how each of these brain patterns was unique. Telling that to an auditorium full of attentive brain scientists. In his casual blue and yellow preppie way making clear that the onetime-only "I" called Bethany Mayhall had never existed before and could never exist again.

My sandwich stuck in my throat.

In the booth behind us, a pair of students argued loudly, apparently about a film script.

"You must take out the suicide at the end."

"If I take out the suicide there's no point to it."

"Well, then, take out the hysterical weeping of the mother."

"She feels very guilty—"

"I'm saying take out the uncontrolled weeping. It has to be reduced in sound. Don't you see?"

We found it difficult not to laugh, so that the diversion was a help. It broke the tension of our talk; cut through the undercurrents. We smiled across the table, older, wiser, finding it pleasantly unlike life: the optional suicide, the disposable lachrymose mother.

For old times' sake, we split a piece of apple pie.

⚭ ⑥ ⚭

Then there was Jay, when we turned the corner on the second floor of the Life Sciences Building. He was dressed in more of a scientist-in-the-lab way than Douglas, blue work shirt and corduroy trousers, heavy leather belt and serious leather hiking boots. His thick brush mustache was the same brown as the cords. He had that quick way of moving I associated with younger men—although it might be he'd move that same way at eighty. Nice thought.

"Hi," I greeted him. "Aren't you the diabetic?"

"And you're the lady with the juicy fruit?"

Chewing gum? No, are you? We laughed at the same time, while my husband looked on, baffled.

Jay said, "I've got you meeting with the other panel members over lunch, Doug. That'll give you four a chance to divide up your territory. After the panel, I've reserved us a court. Where's your racquet?"

"In the car—"

"I thought you were flaking out, old man."

"You hoped so, you upstart." Douglas grinned. He liked having a tennis buddy. He liked the idea of himself playing sports with friends. That small bespectacled boy with the mirror still looked out of his eyes at his reflection, wondering at the blond jock he'd become.

"Follow me," Jay instructed.

"I just ate lunch, with Nan," Douglas reported, not sure of the protocol. "At the Burgher King."

"You can tell them all what to say, then, while they feed their faces. I set this up so I can whisk your wife away for a Ben and Jerry's. I owe her a dessert."

"She just had—" Douglas stopped, hearing himself about to speak for me, to explain we'd shared a strudel. "*That's* why you put me on the program twice," he recovered quickly.

"I've also got you down doing a seminar from nine until midnight. You got any problem with that?"

The men laughed together.

I watched the way Jay had made that happen. The way he pretended to pretend that there were sexual overtones to the scene. Showing off for the other man's wife. Saying, Look at me walk along the fence on my hands. Look at me take you off and away from your husband and tell him even while I'm doing it.

"My place or the elevator?" Jay asked as soon as we were alone. He'd got Douglas together with the other panelists and sent them on their way to the faculty dining room. Saying, as he took my arm for them to see, "So long, guys, don't rush." More laughter.

"I think maybe the elevator," I said, feeling his fingers

touching my skin. "I think so, definitely. The trouble with your place is there won't be anybody else there."

"You like an audience?"

"—I don't know, when a man gets a woman alone in his place, no matter how good his intentions are, his basic nature takes over—"

"And—" He was enjoying this.

"And he can't help himself. He says, 'Would you mind, dear, running two loads of laundry through while I shave?' And then he says, 'And could you get the tires rotated on the BMW while I'm in the shower?' "

"That's not been my experience," Jay countered, pushing ground floor and running his hand down the back of my kelly green T-shirt. "My experience is, you get a woman alone in your place and she says, 'Now if you move the davenport—' "

"Davenport? Nobody says davenport."

"—the divan—"

"Divan?" I turned to him, smiling, standing about three inches away.

" '—the settee over here, and re-cover the wing chairs, and maybe get new drapes. What do you think?' she says."

"My mom would have asked to see your breadbox."

"You were raised by a sugar junkie. I could tell you came from a troubled home."

"Could you?" I leaned into his hand, sorry when the elevator stopped, the door opened, and here we were on the ground floor of the Life Sciences Building, back in the much too real world.

"Will you walk me to the admissions office?" I asked him.

"Did we do it?"

"We got cold feet."

He stopped on the sidewalk in the sun. "Did you used to

sit with the guys under the trees when you were an under-
graduate?"

"There weren't many in my part of Texas."

"Trees."

"Right."

"How about over there?" He led the way to the shade of a
maple. We had the entire campus, it looked like, to ourselves;
this was a serious student body.

Jay took off his shoes and I did the same. Sock hop.

It made me sad, made my chest hurt, that there was no
such thing as casual sex anymore. No way anymore that you
could fling open your arms and legs and then get up and go
home. At our crossroads, too much was at stake; it was too
risky. First we'd lay claim to one another, then we'd start to
expect something in return. We'd be needy and want more,
more of each other. The two of us in bed would become one
more place where things could go awry. Where it could be my
fault. Or his.

I wasn't sure, but I thought his cheeks were wet. Jokers
like us were always laughing to scare away the boogeyman. I
wondered what he was needing so bad, where he was coming
from, but at the same time I didn't want to know. It was the
way strangers sat together on a cold day in a museum coffee
shop. There was that moment of intimacy, but you weren't
going home together. Things didn't have to be okay; neither
of you had to be okay for the other.

"Tell me about the time you played hooky from school,"
I said.

"*The* time?"

"Representative time."

He pulled out a handkerchief from his pocket and blew
his nose. He cleared his throat. "I showed up for the first day

of class, one of those disasters called civics or social studies
or social civics. They herded a bunch of sections into one big
drafty crammed room. My sixth grade being the one that came
headlong into the breech birth of the open classroom. While
Miss Whoever was droning, I attempted to figure out if one of
her earrings was a hearing aid. After while, I started to gag real
loud, like I was going to puke on the indoor-outdoor carpet
of the crazy space. When I got outside"—he pulled up a blade
of grass, as if to chew it, then changed his mind —"I walked
down to this pizza joint and played the jukebox till last period. I didn't have enough money for that and a slice, too."

"What'd you play?" I leaned back on my elbows, pretending I was in high school.

"Ben E. King? The Righteous Brothers? It's gone—" He
put his hands behind his head, maybe also pretending. "How
about you?"

I sat up straight, rolling away the years. Nan Palmer, age
eleven. "Same sort of trick," I said. "I was in sixth grade—
how I hated sixth grade, because by that time girls were supposed to be girls and boys were supposed to be boys. It was
Gender Recognition Year. And here I was still dressing like
Out Our Way in my jeans and baseball cap. And this mutiny
was getting filtered back to my mom—who got her head out
of the cake tin and trotted me down to the big local department store in Round Rock, Texas, and bought me seven
dresses." I smoothed my kelly green linen skirt, demonstrating. "Anyway, this one day, when all the dress stuff was frying
my brain and we were studying the geography of the Lone
Star State, about which I already knew seventeen times more
than Mr. Whatsit, I went up front and said to him in a stage
whisper, 'Uh, excuse me, I'm spotting my dress, would you
mind looking?' And I turned around and stuck my fanny in
his direction. Naturally, he became fire engine red, and said if

I liked, I might be excused to go see the school nurse. I went to the little kids' playground and swung on the swing until school was out. Wishing I was grown up and in Alaska."

We were silent, two public school kids under the trees during recess.

Finally, I rose. "I have to go."

"I seem to be putting on a conference."

"I wish—"

"Gets harder, doesn't it?" he said.

"Gets too hard."

He looked at his watch, and we put on our shoes. Before he walked me across the campus, he put his hands up in front of his chest, elbows bent, and I did the same. And we clasped hands in that way, as though it was some sort of clubhouse grip.

"Come again," he offered.

"In another life," I said.

෴   ⑥   ෴

I took a quick glance at the state map retrieved from Douglas's tidy map compartment, returned it. The route to the salt quarry and the creek was clearer in my mind's eye than anything on the much-folded guide. I'd just wanted some reminder of how far the distance was up along Lake Cayuga to the highway—which on the map looked like a length of green string—connecting Syracuse and Buffalo. I remembered it as an hour's drive, but then I didn't know if my excitement of twenty-three years ago had exaggerated the distance or had exaggerated my speed.

I was almost out of town when I gave in to a nagging fret and went back to a pharmacy I'd passed, for insect repellent. Squatting to pee by the stream that long-ago afternoon, my worry had been whether I was polluting the watershed. No more modest now, my worry was Lyme tick disease in the steamy start-of-summer weather. The near quarter of a century since I'd been here, not even a blink for my fossils, in human terms a third of a normal life span, was, in terms of disease, countless generations. Where had the deer tick, no bigger than a pencil lead's dot, been in those days? It was as if it had just appeared by spontaneous generation, like a smoldering fire in old paint-soaked rags. Where, for that matter, had the AIDS virus appeared from? And cholera, as gone and forgotten as the bustle and butter churn, now back and spreading? Where had it been, the plague, dormant as Dracula in his box with a stake through the heart?

Back when Douglas stayed up half of every night working on his dissertation, pulling together the supporting lab work to show the parallel developments of the memory system and the immune system, we would have talked about all this. He would have had ideas of his own.

How the body knew what was itself and what was not. How the mind knew what had happened to it before and what had not. You couldn't have an immune system which didn't "remember"; rejection of "them" depended on remembering what was "us." And you couldn't have memory without an immune system, because something had to show you what was you that had had the experience and what was not. How could you reproduce if you didn't know what was you and what wasn't? How could you ax the enemy?

I had to smile at the thought: the start of love and war. Love, the product of memory; war, the product of immunology.

In the old days, we would have talked half the night about such ideas. Back when we were both students, were both Texas kids plugging away in the cold wind howling off Lake Michigan, sitting up half the night over black coffee. Then he

would never have said to me, That's not your field. Then he
was glad for willing ears and fresh insight.

Starting up the narrow county road, the air felt cooler.
How beautiful this lake-fingered land was. How grand it was
to be at the wheel. For someone reared by the travel-phobic,
I'd often thought, it seemed a cruel fate which had placed me
in a faux British valley of church spires and old homes, with
few roads leading in and a pitiful few leading out.

In those old tomboy rockhound days, I'd been ready to die
for wheels. It hadn't seemed fair that grown-ups who never
wanted to go anywhere, period, had cars, plural, at their beck
and call. Two in our driveway, as a case in point. I'd constantly had to tease, wheedle, or cajole my mom to take me
up to Marble Falls or Burnet, someplace where the near-core
of the earth lay on the surface of Texas. I'd used all manner of
pretty shoddy tricks, playing on her incessant mourning for all
her miscarried babies. "If you had eight kids, Mom, you'd be
carpooling them to Little League and ballet and scout troops
and Sunday School picnics. Think about it," I'd say. "All you
have to do with me is take a thermos of lemonade and a bunch
of hems to mend, and that's it. Dad always works on Satur-
day. Come on, Mom."

It didn't seem fair when explorers like me, who wanted to
go everywhere—to see those trilobites as big as alley cats in
South America, those look-alike fossils in Wales—were without vehicles. Explorers like me who longed to go to any and all
islands, with their cut-off worlds of different animals and different rocks. I'd had a mad desire to go to Hawaii to see what
islands were made of that had risen and gone under and risen
again from the sea. And to the Poles, North and South. Find
out if there were ice sheets both places, and what was under
them. To go to the deserts and find out what dry air preserved.

I used to turn the globe on my geography teacher's desk,

big blue-oceaned, intricately labelled world globe, and want to dig down under the apple peel of its surface to see what was there, knowing, which my teacher didn't happen to, that 99.5 percent of the earth wasn't habitable land. I remembered spinning the globe while he, lanky man with a pot belly and straggly hair, roused himself and shooed me away, saying it was his off period, and shouldn't I be somewhere else?

Busy with daydreaming, I overshot the turnoff to the green-string highway, and had to pull the car around on a side road and head back. It was no longer a dirt road with a quarry sign at the corner. Now the road was paved, and a boxy windowless building which said SENECA STORAGE blocked the view of the quarry entrance. The change rattled me.

Perhaps they'd shut down the salt mining. Dammed the stream or bulldozed it over. Put a boat dock where the old water wheel had turned. Poured the foundations of trendy condos on the fossilized imprints of the past. I couldn't shake loose the idea that if such were the case, if this particular paleontology field-trip site were gone, then so was any chance I might have to start over.

My hands grew damp on the wheel. My breath came in short bursts as if I was running. I'd stopped by the admissions office to pick up a course catalogue—Jay had shown me the way. "Do you have time to rotate the tires on my car?" he'd asked. "That wing chair of yours needs re-covering," I'd told him. We were back to joking. Next year's catalogue wasn't out yet, but I'd left my name. Not saying that being just one year behind would be progress for me. This year's was beside me on the seat; degree programs warming my skin through my skirt.

The quarry entrance was still there, marked with a company sign and another which said NO TRESPASSING. I turned off—too nervous even to slow down. I could hear the rumbling truck sounds and relief flooded through me. If they were still mining the salt which looked like dingy clay, then they were still going down into the ground, unearthing earth, and so could I.

By the time someone took notice of me, and a burly guy got out of a green truck the size of a one-story building, I had done a U-turn and was heading back to the road. I'd wanted to stand at the rim and gaze down into the carved-out canyon. Imagine early miners, early fossil-hunters, riding down on mule-back, bags strapped to their saddles, lifting out specimens with the tenderest of care—taking them to the big labelled drawers at the nearby Paleontology Museum.

The paved access road stopped at the shore of Lake Cayuga. And, to my joy, the old water wheel and mill were still there, though in such a state of disrepair it was a wonder they hadn't fallen over into a pile of planks. On the left, the creek flowed to the lake, undamned, undredged, looking just as it had so many years before.

I pressed my hand to my chest. It was not too late. It wasn't. There was all the time left that I needed. Human time, which went so fast or so slow depending on your vantage point—you were the butterfly starting off to school with the boy, gone when he came home, or you were the Galapagos turtle coming home from your first day of school when the boy was a bearded old man—was still time enough. For humans.

I took the disposable diaper pack and my assortment of picks and crossed the road. The place was so deserted I didn't even lock the car. All I wanted was one specimen. A part of a specimen: a bit of tail, shield, helmet. Just something to take home as talisman. So that when I awoke, when I returned to my old life, I would have it there, could touch it, would know that I had not dreamed today.

I crouched in the cold spring water, feet bare, and ran my

hands gently over the black slate ledges of the banks. Then walked upstream, careful of fallen sticks, careful of sharp rocks. The stream came downhill in a series of spills—you couldn't call them waterfalls by any stretch, but spills, like pouring a bowlful of water on the top step of a stairway and watching it roll down.

At the third rise, the going got too rocky. The water deeper. I stepped back one level and bent close to the bank. With care, I pulled out a layer of rock, as if slipping one block out from a tower of building blocks.

Back by the car, I settled the layered slab of the papery shale, which was about the size of a shirt box, and, using a flat knife, lifted the top layer off. I could see fern imprints, and sighed with relief. I had not forgotten how. I hadn't a magnifying glass with me, but could see tiny shells such as were still found on the Gulf Coast at home. There might be a *Phacops rana* tail, but I couldn't be sure. Something would be there, if not a whole specimen, at least a part of one.

And this time, when I was working at the table, my damp black shale spread out all around me, it would not be my turn to put the work aside, climb the stairs, and make a baby.

It was while I was packing my finds between layers of disposable diapers in the trunk of the car that last summer's vacation came back to me.

All of it. As if finally handling the fossils I had hoped to find then had unearthed all that my disappointment and the later upheaval had buried.

We had gone to Blue Mountain Lake in the Adirondacks, just as Douglas had said when he recounted our trip. Then we'd gone north to Tupper Lake. Bert and I were studying the quadrants of the USGS maps we'd brought along. His mind was on gorges. We could take a state road and find the source of the Hudson River, he proposed to his dad. Way up here, see? And then, a short dirt-road drive more and he could do a dive in the tricky Opalescent Gorge. I looked over his shoulder, fascinated that there was a spot called Flowed Lands. Could that be volcanic? Or, Bert had suggested, if we went farther toward the east, into the Sawtooth Mountain area, there was Panther Gorge. And Ausable Chasm.

Or, if we went on to Lake Placid, took the short ferry ride across Lake Champlain at Essex, the guidebook promised us a dozen species of trilobites and, an hour away, the treacherous waters of Huntington Gorge. "Wahoo," Bert said. "Take a look at this!" "This" being a warning that some dozen and a half people had died in Huntington, which had swift rapids and corkscrew caves. What an enticement.

I was reading about *Bathynotus*, which I'd never seen, thought to have buried its eggs in the mud like a horseshoe crab. Not that anyone knew, of course, how trilobites reproduced themselves. Or knew why, I thought—looking at the glossy plate of a blind agnostid—their vision ranged from seeing in all directions to being sightless. Or which came first in time, or if these were parallel developments.

A longing had come over me to be back in school again, debating just such matters. Arguing with my teachers that it was not the way Darwin had said at all, that things changed gradually, randomly, without organization, without direction, mutating like a leaf picked up from other leaves in a sudden gust and dropped somewhere else. Arguing that species changed rapidly, suddenly, overnight. A continent shifted, a sea dried up, a predator moved in.

A longing to be back digging into a world before there

were humans, or birds wading or skimming, before there were the oceans we knew now, or men and women and marriage and offspring. Before there was even sexual reproduction. Before there were minds. Oh, yes, I was thinking, especially back before there were minds.

The only thing I knew for sure since starting life out as an academic wife was that I was on the wrong track. And not all the intervening years and rewriting of memory could erase that certainty.

"Come on, Dad," Bert said. "Let's do that. Go on up to Champlain. Mom can do what she used to do."

"Can't you read?" Douglas had asked, pointing to the warning message. "You'll get yourself killed yet with your scuba diving—"

Bethany had instantly risen to her brother's defense, fussing at her dad for calling their brother's passion for diving, for human breathing, "scuba diving" when Bert had said about a million times that he was a scientific, not a recreational, diver, that he was already doing extended-range diving, that cave diving was not for tourists, that he was becoming a marine physiologist, not a guide to Flipper. That his dad was a deaf-mute asshole—well, that not to his face. "Daa-aad," Bethany, loyal sibling in her pink biker's shorts, had wailed, "not *scuba*—"

I was sitting, listening, lacing my hiking boots tighter, looking out east toward Mount Marcy, the highest point in New York State, a low fifty-three hundred plus. Thinking that the Adirondacks were tired mountains, once high as the sky, now lower even than the lowest meadows of the Rockies, three times lower than the highest peak in Alaska, that youth of mountains.

I was trying also to swallow my anger at my husband. I'd looked away from the brightness of the sun, focusing on the sight of some ancient glacier's path below. Angry because

Douglas always did that—relegated our passions to hobbies.
Scuba diving. Fossil collecting. As if he was saying bungee
diving or mushroom picking. It was an old sore spot between
us. Once when we were arguing I'd hollered at him, "And
what do you call what you do? Mind fucking?"

That afternoon, I collected myself and commented on
Huntington Gorge. "It does look dangerous."

"Don't be a Nanny Mom," Bethany chided me, glad to have
a chance to scold her parents equally. "They're *his* lungs—"
I could see her as if I was still sitting on that rock, tying my
boot. Doing her leg thrusts, in a skinny pink T with a black
muscle shirt over it, her biking shorts, running shoes. Her hair,
usually loose, in the braid she wore for hiking, and a sweatband around her forehead. Saying Mom, Dad, Bert. Come on,
be nice. Don't say that. Treat each other gentle. Please don't
fight. Being the peacemaker, the peacekeeper of the family.

"—It's my neck," Bert agreed, raising his voice. He had
the maps in his hand, waving them. When he got a thing in
his mind he didn't let it go; he was like a dog hanging on to a
bone. "Come on, Dad," he said. "Wahoo."

Douglas seemed to tremble he got so mad. Face red to
the roots of his hair. He grabbed the maps and flung them to
the ground. "Okay, fine, great," he said. "Go. Let's go. IT'S
YOUR NECK. BREAK IT IF YOU WANT TO." The last
rising to a shout.

"Daa-aad!" Bethany looked stricken. "He didn't mean it,"
she said to Bert, turning quickly to her brother, who stood
looking down at the maps, stunned.

"Gee, Dad, I didn't know you cared," our son said, trying
for a light tone.

"It's clear *you* don't," Douglas snapped, and strode off
down the trail, whistling, not looking back.

I could hear the tune again, the same tune I'd heard the

morning I asked him about the trip and he'd gone over the map lines of the week like a tour guide. Doubtless not even aware that he was repeating the sound track from a very bad time.

We hadn't taken the ferry across Champlain after all. I didn't find the blind trilobite or the one that buried its eggs in the mud. Bert didn't get trapped in a whirlpool in Huntington Gorge (although we read later of someone who did). We drove westward instead, saw a great lake, ate at an okay resort, all four finding reasons why we needed to get back home.

Bert moved in with Alison in the fall and became scarcer than sunshine in February in Mead's Mill. His dad never mentioned the trip again.

When we got the terrible news about Bethany, I saw Douglas's face when I repeated the word "accident" over the phone. And even though he knew his son wasn't in Texas and his daughter was, he turned white as dough and I knew his words came back to him.

The next day, when I finally located Bert to tell him, he said, "Sis? Jesus, not *Sis*."

We had all been looking in the wrong direction.

When I got back to the Ithaca campus, an hour, no, more like three, later, I could see Douglas a block away walking down the main drag. I'd told Jay, his tennis partner, to tell him that I'd be in front of the Burgher King at six o'clock, in time to attend the evening's reception.

Dusty, grungy, I hardly looked the part of a conference speaker's wife. I still had on the baseball cap, THE baseball cap, from several millennia ago, before the slow-silting deposits of married time. It was orange and had a (faint, faded) Longhorn on it. Now more a smudge with legs. I'd tucked my cork-heeled sandals under the front seat and had on my sturdiest hiking shoes. Sunblock streaked my skin. My hair was a tumbleweed. My hands were black-rock grimy.

Before I left the site, I'd lifted one more shirt-box-size hunk of the wet shale and packed it with infinite care on the floor of the backseat behind me. It had been grand to use my picks and probes and slicers and tweezers again for their original purpose, after years of employing them to remove splinters from the kids, cut package twine, pry open paint cans.

I waved out the window. "Hey," I said, parallel-parking in two swift motions and getting out of the car.

"Where have you been?"

"Didn't Jay tell you?"

"He claimed all you said was you'd meet me here." He looked frazzled, the brain scientist. His yellow preppie shirt damp under the arms, his denim-blue cotton jacket hanging by a finger over his shoulder. Tennis racquet in one hand, his locker bag in the other.

I'd forgotten my having wheels meant he was without.

"That's all I told him." I locked the car and tucked my spare key in my handbag. "I owe you half a tank of gas," I said. "I guess I'm a mess. Where are we quartered? I'd better clean up." I looked around, as if our accommodations were wedged between the Burgher King and JoJo's FroYo.

"He said," Douglas began in a measured tone, "he said that he left you at the admissions office four hours ago." His face was definitely unhappy.

"That sounds about right." I looked down at my quartz watch, amazed at the orderly passage of clock time.

"Tell me," Douglas said, dropping his gym bag and grabbing my arm. "Where did you go?"

I felt the chill wind of an upcoming fight hit my midsection.

Which did nothing to dampen my spirits in the least. "Unhand me," I said in a friendly tone.

He let go of my arm. "Jay's got us down the street at a Ramada." He picked up his bag, the racquet under his arm.

"You want to drive?" I asked.

He didn't move. "You planned this," he accused. "You brought your keys."

"I had them with me." I shrugged.

"When you didn't show up for the panel—"

"You don't like me listening to you and your pals."

"Not once have I ever said that." He put on his jacket, straightened his tie, and stepped to the curb.

"Inferred, often. Because if I listen to you, then I am inclined to want to talk about the subject, have my own ideas. And it's *not my field*."

"What are you doing, Nan? What?" He pulled me closer so he could lower his voice.

What? Claiming what should have been mine all along? Getting a life? Trying to pick up the pieces and go on? "I went by the lakeshore, Douglas. Along Cayuga. Past the salt quarry."

He took two long strides and peered in the car window. The empty box of disposable diapers was on the backseat. The stacks of packed shale, neat as a layer cake, on the floor. What else did he see? Insect repellent. The toes of my cork-soled shoes. The course catalogue on the front seat.

This time he flung his tennis gear on the sidewalk and grabbed me by the shoulders, shaking me until my baseball hat fell to the sidewalk.

He yelled, for the benefit of any and every college student on bike or Rollerblades who happened by, "DO YOU HEAR ME? IF YOU DO THIS AGAIN, IF YOU SET ME UP

THIS WAY AGAIN, I SWEAR I'LL SEND YOU BACK
TO ROUND ROCK, TEXAS, WHERE YOU BELONG."

I bent to retrieve my cap. "I remembered our vacation last
summer," I said. "The one that didn't end up at Hungtington
Gorge."

He crumpled before my eyes. "Don't," he said. "Please."

"We're going to be late for the reception."

6

The beaches of Sanibel and Captiva islands moved not only with the tides but with the ravages of Gulf storms. Hurricane Agnes in '72 had wiped out a stretch of trees between the bay and the ocean. Blown-in sand had raised the shoreline. Sometimes there was no pass at all between the islands—sometimes a veritable ship channel. It was geology happening in observable time.

Although of course you knew that the soft slopes of the Alleghenies and Adirondacks were wearing down, shedding grade and ground, it was impossible on those weary weathered rises to see change. In contrast, here my daily stroll was a brief sun-streaked reminder that today was not the same as yesterday.

The children had come for the weekend, and now I was due for a visit from Douglas. "I assume it's my turn," he'd said in a grim tone on the phone, "to make the trip." I was missing them in direct proportion to how much I was dreading seeing him.

The continued rain had determined who showed up on my shoreline. I missed a chordate I hadn't seen at all on this wet trip, the tunicate, who appeared in the mudflats on the inlet's edge when the water level was down. A creature who went from vertebrate when young to invertebrate when grown, startling as a tadpole becoming a frog, and who looked to the casual beachcomber like a star-crusted oven mitt. Yesterday, after the kids left, I'd rowed to the mangroves, dropping shrimp overboard to watch the flat striped sheepshead lunge for its lunch, a frequent tagalong when the water was high. Today everyone was feasting on the beach. The wood storks shuffling their red feet in the shallow tidewater to rustle up small crabs, the yellow-legged white ibis striking with its yellow beak.

Bert had been sunk in gloom because of the statewide flooding, the semester over and his time free and all the caves unsafe. Georgia and north Florida getting night and day drenchings, the worst flooding in sixty-five years. A federal disaster area just when he'd had time and a bit of money put away to log some major hours, test a new rebreather, under water.

The Apalachicola, the Chipola, the Choctawhatchee rivers, all out of their banks. On the Georgia-Florida border the dam at Lake Seminole, which normally handled 15,000 cubic feet a second, was getting 242,000 cubic feet. A regular Niagara. Naturally, Bert had complained, all those field ponds of his were now just sunk into the general marsh, the ooze of that part of the state. Turbulent underground undertows and sudden whooshes, virtual rolling rivers under standing water.

We'd sat at the table on the dining chairs covered with so many coats of white paint it was like sitting on plastic. Finishing up fat banana pancakes—my attempt to replicate Jesse's recipe, not quite succeeding—while Bert grumbled that there wasn't anything else to do and he thought he'd take a dive at Little Salt Springs, the no-oxygen cave-filled pool up the road from me.

"Oolite and Key Largo limestone," I read from a flyer he'd brought me about the off-limits sinkhole. "Saber-tooth tiger teeth."

We'd started laughing about that, saying "saber-teeth tiger's tooth" and "tiger-tooth saber teeth," the kids having had a little wine since they were in no hurry to hit the road.

"Let's shove," Bert said at last, getting up. "I guess I should have called the atmospheric science guys and got some kind of permission, just to cover my ass. What do you think?" He addressed Alison.

"Remember those squawking birds like something out of a horror film? They must be grounded, their oily feathers soaked."

"Maybe," Bert said, gathering up their packs, "I'll see a roasted turtle with saber-tooth teeth in his leg and a boomerang older than Australia's boomerang around his neck, and I can write it up for the *Geographic*."

Alison had looked less like Bethany to me this time. And at first I was certain that this was a conscious kindness on the young diver's part. Deciding that she'd put on a brighter shade of lipstick than my daughter would have worn, had donned a formfitting hot pink T in intentional contrast to the usual faded shirts the girls had both favored. But then I'd looked away, shutting my eyes against such foolishness. It was all in my mind—an attempt to see this helpful gentle person not as a resemblance, an echo, but as herself.

(All the while my body fighting the ache her very presence caused.)

Yesterday, after a suppertime feast of Dungeness crab

legs, Bert had showed me diagrams of a mineral mountain two miles undersea, the mountain itself a volcanic basalt dome. He'd showed me—sketching quickly—how black smoke over 600 degrees poured out of the formation, but how the surrounding water couldn't boil because of the immense pressure. The range growing even as we speak, he told me, its extrusions hot enough to melt lead and yet with springs which were home to anemones and sightless shrimp.

Alison in her pink T had reminded him that people couldn't dive down there where it was that hot. That they had robots from Japan and the U.S. that went down and sent back reports. Robots carrying sensors and recorders and monitoring cameras and retrieving equipment. The same way they sent a robot down into the volcano on the earth's surface, they were sending them down into the volcanoes undersea.

"Robots." Bert complained amiably that every time he talked about anything, Alison switched the subject to robots. He bet she was seeing R2-D2 on the sly.

"No," she teased, "I've got it for Dante II, he has *eight legs*." She rolled her eyes and crossed her thighs and made extravagant kissing noises.

"All right, all right," Bert had moaned. He never got mad at Alison. His earlier girlfriends hadn't known how to jolly him the way she did. "But somebody has to interpret the data, don't they?"

"—Sinkai 6500 is sort of cute, too," Alison added. "Definitely brainy."

"Quit."

Now, when I came in, the phone was ringing and I almost didn't answer it. I needed to pee, and, besides, it was probably Douglas. Cancelling his trip or giving me the flight time. Either way, nothing I was in a hurry to hear.

"It's me," came a strong voice on the line.

"Alison?"

"Listen, Nan, don't get scared, this is absolutely nothing really, not the bends or anything like that. I don't want you—"

"Bert?" I slid, phone in hand, to the floor.

"A piece of a ledge fell on his gas regulator, and he had to surface in a hurry. He must've got a bubble. I'm using the car phone to get a copter and check him out at the hyperbaric chamber in Sarasota. That's routine. He'd break my jaw if I didn't do it like you're supposed to. But you're totally not to worry—"

I felt the sunny room go dark. It was always this way; had been this way in November. You were watching the front door of the saloon for the guy in the black hat when you heard the gun being cocked behind your back. *Bert.*

"It may take twenty-four hours, but I'm definitely positive—"

"Is there somewhere I can call?" My voice sounded like it was coming from a deep hole.

"I gotta go—I'll check back with you later. You are positively not to worry."

I looked at my feet, which were still attached to my bare legs, trying to recall what the kids had told me about their last abortive trip to Little Salt Springs. How they'd picked four locks, or unwound four chains. How a hundred ospreys had come screeching down out of the trees like something out of a Hitchcock movie. That there were NO TRESPASSING signs everywhere. And a van. A ranger van? That, whatever, Bert had called it off.

I hadn't reacted this morning when he'd said, I should have okayed it with someone at the atmospheric science lab at U. Miami. I hadn't registered that he'd be diving without a backup, Alison aboveground as they had only one rebreather for the anoxic water. It had sounded safe as a bathtub, more like an archeological tourist attraction, see the sloth bones, the mastodon tusks, go down in a glass-bottom boat so no one can exhale or inhale in the oxygen-free pond. The taking of photographs permitted.

My mind had been distracted, trying not to think that they'd soon be gone. Trying not to get into a stew because Douglas had scheduled his arrival for after their departure. The only available cheap flight, he'd insisted. And perhaps he thought we needed to be alone. But still— And now I'd be meeting him with this fright hanging over us.

I stood stock-still by the back door, numb for some length of time, trying to remember what I was supposed to be doing.

I kept replaying the afternoon we'd heard about Bethany. We were at the house on Stone Hollow Road, getting ready to have Thanksgiving dinner with our friends. Who? Big crowd. Winifred and her husband were to be there (or was he already dead?). Deans and maybe the provost. A bountiful New England buffet we never ate.

Douglas had got the phone and handed it to me, because it was Jesse. He always did that, let me do the talking first, get the conversation going, then he'd pitch in a greeting and hand it back to me. Jesse, I'd assumed, would want to let us know our daughter was safely there. Tell us who else she was feeding at the big ranch table. There would be some mention of Daddy Mayhall's absence, which was partly for Douglas's sake.

"Wait—" Jesse was saying in a wild tone when I put the phone to my ear. "Doug, wait—"

"Jess?"

"Jesus, God, Nan, it's the worst news in the world I've got for you and that stepson of mine. You want to sit yourself down. Tell him he isn't going to be able to take it standing up. Tell Doug to lift the receiver in the living room, and you stay on. Hear? I'm not going to be able to say the words twice."

I motioned for Douglas, sitting as I did so, my feet turned to rubber. That terror that begins on the scalp and crawls down the spine to the pit of the stomach had its cold hold on me. "Accident?" I said. "Is she—"

"*Bethany?*" I heard Douglas say, in some stranger's voice.

And then, somehow, we were on a plane.

This morning Bert had been talking buoyancy compensation, and I'd said, "Every diver is a Cartesian diver." I was remembering the science demonstration of the bottle with the rubber membrane and an inverted tube of air inside called a Cartesian diver. Proof of Boyle's law, my teacher had explained, that gas volume is compressible but water volume is not. I'd realized that every diver would prove the law just as well: that even a naked diver would begin to sink when lung air was compressed.

"How do you know that stuff?" he had asked me.

It had hit me wrong. Now even my son, I'd decided, on the defensive, thought I was setting foot in *his* field. Damn them, I thought. "Even though I went to public school, sonny," I'd snapped, "I learned a few tidbits of knowledge."

"What's her problem?" Bert had turned, bemused, to Alison.

"You?" The kindly girl had laughed, defusing the moment.

I knew what it could mean, Bert's gas regulator damaged by a falling fragment of rock, his having to surface too fast. Embolisms, air bubbles to the spine, successive weeks of treatment with little result if things didn't right themselves at once.

Brushing my hair from my eyes, or whatever was getting between me and seeing, I stepped out back and let loose the sea hare I'd caught in the bucket. Watching as its languid brown and silvery wings carried it out of sight. I'd meant to compare its hidden coil with a shell I'd brought back from Cayuga: perhaps a distant cousin. Entranced anew by the idea that all fossil shells had once been merely vestigial ornaments on vast, soft floating creatures. That the animals had wrapped themselves around the structures; had never been contained by them. Bert had always liked to reach his hand in and find the hidden coiled shell in the soft folds.

In the side yard, a blue heron was picking its fragile stilty legs up and gingerly setting them down. Birds didn't know. They had their young in eggs. Some hatched. Some flew off. Some didn't do either. Was that elegant sleek-beaked creature taking an inventory of its offspring? Not even a conceivable concept.

Apparently I fainted. Or else I simply decided to stretch out on the grass on my back with one leg under me until I broke out into a clammy sweat, sickened with nausea. There were a hundred billion nerve cells tended by a trillion support cells in each brain making more connections than there were constellations in the universe.

And no two of them alike.

☜   ⑥   ☜

On the car radio going to the airport, I listened to stories about the deluge. Apalachicola Bay's oyster harvesting halted. I didn't even know where that was, or that you ate Gulf oysters. I'd thought of Bert, exhilarated in spite of himself at the idea of the anoxic dive. The thrill was always there for divers, whatever he argued. They didn't dive for saber teeth, they dived because there were so few places left to explore.

I got to the airport early, dressed as if for church, but I didn't mind hanging out. It was a familiar limbo with well-established guidelines. Everyone had been through it at one time or another. Your flight was cancelled; all flights were cancelled. Nothing was moving but the crowd. Hundreds of you milled about, people out of their shoes, ankles swollen, backs aching, no food too dreadful to keep you from eating. Old grannies in those boatlike corrective shoes reading *Penthouse*; CEOs in tailor-made suits reading the recipes in *Redbook*. Everyone telling what dire consequences the delay was causing. And nothing to do but wait it out.

Douglas, stepping through the gate, looked older, drawn. His hair had grown out and was graying. Driving toward the causeway and the two islands, I told him about the call, trying to repeat Alison's reassurances: Definitely, absolutely, positively we were not to worry.

It rendered us speechless all the way to the oystershell driveway at the cottage.

It was strange, being alone with Douglas here at Sanibel. Just the two of us, in this much-painted, wind-snug, sunset-rouged room. He'd always disliked the place in direct proportion to my love for it. Perhaps because Daddy Mayhall still inhabited its halls and walls.

There was no message on the phone; it had not rung since we got back. It made sense that we were not to rush up the road to the hyperbaric chamber at Sarasota; the girl didn't need to be also worrying about how to reach us on the coastal highway. Still, it made us brittle with each other, waiting. The fresh coffee was growing cold.

"So where the hell was he?" Douglas asked, for the second time.

"Place called Little Salt Springs."

"Where he wasn't supposed to be."

"Something like that." I hadn't given him all the details, feeling guilty I hadn't insisted Bert call the marine science people at Miami.

He read the folder that Bert had left. "Proboscideans—

that means nose, right? Llamas, ground sloths, saber cats." He was reciting as if reading off cue cards. "They mention an ancestor of the Great White Shark." He snorted. "You know these things. They play up the finds and don't tell you two reliable facts about the risk. The sinkhole, in this stamp-sized photo, looks like a molar, with two tap roots. Look, it says over two hundred feet deep. Nan, do you think he got in over his head?"

Douglas did not even hear himself. I said no. I'd said no to other versions of the same question. But of course everyone did that under stress, went over the same two or three facts, asked the same one or two questions. It was a clear day, there was no wind sheer, the pilot sent no distress signal. How could the plane have exploded? You repeated yourself, trying to put a puzzle together with half the pieces missing.

"He told me he was using an enriched air trimix, a mix of helium, nitrogen, and oxygen that divers had tested specifically for that kind of pond. And a rebreather," I repeated.

"He must have gone down too deep." He threw the folder away in frustration.

"I told you Alison said something hit the tank. Apparently there is a ledge—" I'd said this before also. "He was intending just to take a quick look, that's why he didn't check it out with anyone. He told me he wasn't interested in—beast bones." Using Bert's phrase, my voice cracked.

"His usual caves were flooded, is that it?"

"Yes. All of north Florida is under water." Why did Douglas make me feel somehow responsible. We had not done that with Bethany. Had not asked, Why did you let her go? Why did you let her rent a car? Why didn't you go with her? I guess the shock wiped out everything else.

I fixed us fresh-tuna sandwiches with tomato slices. Dumb on the west coast of Florida to buy fresh tuna. Which you had to fret might be bootleg dolphin. Dumb to stand in the kitchen by the silent phone and assemble the semblance of a meal still in my airport dress. But Douglas, too, was in his public clothes; his tie, red with tiny fir trees on it, still knotted. I wouldn't have been surprised to see a briefcase tucked between his feet.

After a moment of poking at the food, I commented, "You look older."

He said, stung, "How so?"

"Don't I?"

He rubbed his eyes, as if to clear away politeness.

"I can see the stress you're under," he admitted.

"We're not twenty-five, Douglas."

"What is this about, Nan?"

What was it about? I guess I was picking a fight, or offering a distraction. Focusing on something extraneous.

Maybe this was why people got in their cars and trekked off to help disaster victims. It was a short-term crisis, not really yours, and then you were back in your own bed, safe, counting the heads of your kin, feeling grateful. Perhaps I should head for the Florida Panhandle on the border of Georgia, where I could ladle out hot soup to frantic washed-out homeowners who didn't like hot soup when they hadn't lost their houses. Who'd yell at you and then be sorry. And pretty soon you'd be looking at pictures of their prize rhubarb or their dog-show-winning Jack Russell terrier. Pretty soon you'd be eating the soup yourself (it wasn't so bad, sort of greasy, a watery carrot and celery broth).

"We have unfinished business—"

"I'm not seeing her," he said, "if that's what you're asking." He pushed away his sandwich plate.

"No. I guess I was asking how you could even think of starting this all over again."

"If we never married and never parented, we'd have even less to lose," he said drily.

I flinched, but he was right. I nodded. "Yes, all right." Why had I put on this dress? Hospital dress? Alison told us not to worry. "Remember," I said, trying to get a grip on myself, "when we used to take those separate plane flights when they were small?"

"What has that—?"

"Rewriting our wills every time. Leaving the kids first with my parents, then, when they were older, with Jesse on the ranch, then, later, wanting them to stay on in our house, with Doris. How we worried about what would happen to them if they lost us." I stabbed the tuna with a fork, recalling our useless misplaced caution. "We should have spent some time determining what would happen to us if *we* lost *them*."

Douglas made a trip to the bathroom and came back without his shoes. After a minute, he said, "I've been thinking about the day we heard about Walter. My brother."

"You were there?"

"Where? The ranch. Yes." He looked toward the wind-shuttered windows. "My memory is that I was, although you hear a story enough times—yes, I was. In '67, it must have been. I was already in grad school. Well, you know that. The war was all over the news and papers but not much in the classroom, if you remember. I was home, yes, that's right. It must have been spring break."

How could he forget? How could he forget anything? The date, the day, the hour, where he was standing, how the light fell. It must be different if it wasn't your child.

"I can see my dad on the phone." He concentrated, squinting as if getting the scene in focus. "I know in the movies someone in uniform knocks on the door. Perhaps they couldn't find the ranch? All I know is, I can see him on the phone. He's in his cow-pony boots, dirty, he hasn't washed his hands. He's growing redder and redder by the minute, and yelling, 'Are you sure about that, son?' In my memory, Jesse, who is standing there by his side already knows. And I already know. Maybe there had been a letter. Or we guessed."

I brought us a little Scotch, warm, in brandy glasses. Medicinal doses. I didn't want to drink if we were going to have to jump in the car in the middle of the night, but Douglas had grown pale. I thought the slow burn would be instantly helpful, to us both.

"When he got off the phone, Jesse asked him, 'Walt, are you all right?' Words to that effect. She was always worried in those days he was going to have a stroke. Apoplexy, she called it. And my dad bellowed at her, charging like a bull, 'Walter's dead, Walter's dead.' He did look as if he was going to blow a gasket." Douglas considered the drink in his hands, drained it. "I worried over Dad until I forgot how I felt about my brother."

It was easy to imagine what Daddy Mayhall would have done if he'd got the news of a second son in trouble. Torn that ranch house into scraps of two-by-fours and stone rubble. Burned the outbuildings to the ground, herded the fed cattle into some nearby tank. Beat his latest Lincoln to a tin can with a sledgehammer. Somehow we all had more sympathy for those who lost control. Something the rest of us were constrained from doing. The Reverend Mrs. Clayton sitting composed, stitching through an afternoon. Douglas grown gray and haggard. It seemed to me at that moment, looking at him, that any more bad news and he would throw in the towel.

His recalling that long-ago afternoon in the brush country, my recalling the dreadful call on a day we never got to offer thanksgiving, made me wonder what we would remember from this time. If things went wrong. If Alison's positively, absolutely, allowed some margin of error. Would Carole and Jay and all our recent disputes seem trivial and foolish, instantly forgotten, or would they be the life rafts we clung to?

"I don't think I can make it if we lose him," Douglas said.

"We can't," I agreed.

I tried to think of something to say, of something we could do, but nothing came. In the old days, we might have stopped and made love, shut out the world. But, sadly, that too had become unsafe ground. I cleared away the still-filled plates, turned off the coffee. Brought out the bottle of Scotch.

"And now?" Douglas asked. He pushed his glass across the table toward me and put his hands on his knees. He looked winded. When he shifted his stretched-out legs, his khakis seemed tight at the knees.

Now? What was he asking me. Did he think that we would do best to go our separate ways? To make it official? That it was time to quit tearing at each other's flesh and drilling out each other's bones? Time to quit being constant reminders of the past.

"I don't know," I told him. We were all on support systems, we were all under continuous decompression.

"We've talked about a trip to Chicago." He was staring at the windows, as if listening.

"Chicago was a train station for us, wasn't it?" I asked him. "Somewhere we both showed up, on our way to and from somewhere else."

Here we were, Douglas and Nan, speaking again of the large Windy City. The city where we had met, true, but where we'd been together for only two of our twenty-five commingled years. What was it we came back to again and again when we talked of it, Chicago? That we were students? That we were on our own? It was, must be, a nostalgia for that brief stretch of time in which you are primarily neither child of

parents nor parents of children. Just you, full-time student of
that rich, complex, demanding, orderly, rewarding accumula-
tion of everything which was *not you*: school. A brief escape
from the drama of family, that knife plunged to the hilt into
our adult lives.

"You loved it," Douglas said.

"Then, yes—"

"You loved it." He got to his feet, almost angry. "YOU
LOVED THAT CITY." He was nearly shouting. "You cried
when I took the job at Mead's Mill because you missed the city
so badly."

What was he insisting on? That the two of us had once
understood each other? That there had been a time filled
with hope?

I had a sudden empathy for Texas's overgrown aging
football nuts. Back at the game wearing their mums, waving
pennants, screaming their lungs out every first down. Going
back and getting drunk at the fraternity or sorority house,
heading out to the lake, looking for the very spot where they
once necked with their university sweethearts. It wasn't really
that different.

I stood, too, and flung my arm in the air. "Taxi," I shouted,
"taxi," trying to make a joke. But when the door swung open,
I couldn't see my son for the tears.

⟋ ⑥ ⟋

We wanted to surprise you," Alison said, beaming. Her
face streaked, her cherry lipstick eaten away.

"Why didn't you call?" Douglas wheeled around, dis-
believing.

"Hey, Dad. What's this?" Bert was in shorts, his color good, without the puffy, waterlogged appearance that I realized I'd been imagining. "The whole contingent, how about that?"

My knees were weak. Chicago? What on earth had we been talking about. And why. Our nerves chewed down to the nub with worry no matter how much Alison had tried to reassure. "We were—wild," I said, wiping my eyes.

"I told you absolutely it would be okay," the girl said. "The copter came, and by the time we got to Sarasota, he was fine."

"I trained her well," Bert told us. "She did it all by the book."

"You just did that to test me."

I got out the wine for them. Poured more Scotch for us. My head received the good news, but my body was still reeling. I felt kicked as if by a mule; my vision was fuzzy. I couldn't remember where the bottle was and it was sitting right there. The glasses? Out there also. Should I set out cheese? Could Bert eat? Or had he? I couldn't grasp it. He was all right; perfectly fine. Diving was like that: tails you lose, heads you win.

"You gave us quite a scare," Douglas said, visibly restraining himself from lashing out because they hadn't thought to call. He did indeed look older now. He looked wiped out. A father.

"We didn't mean to worry you, I told Nan—" Alison said, her own panic vanished, all but forgotten. A very happy student in a hot pink T.

"I didn't expect to see you, Dad," Bert said. "We thought we might as well crash back here, not do the drive-all-night thing. Were you actually worried about *me*? The *other* kid?"

Douglas stood. He moved his arm as if to take a swing. "Hold it, right there," he said.

Bert lounged on the white-covered couch. "I mean, hey, I'm the one who should have got it the first time, right? I'm the one who was always the wild one, not Sis. Say it, Dad, go on. You wouldn't have been surprised if it had been me who got snuffed." Or sorry, his injured tone suggested.

Douglas flinched. He turned his back, hands clenched into fists. His words of last summer unspoken in the air. "Stop it," he ordered.

"Hey, forget it." Bert waved his wineglass in my direction, for a refill. "I mean, whoa. It's just the bad seed speaking here."

"You have no idea what you're talking about." Douglas moved to the window seat across the room.

"I have a pretty good idea." The boy folded his arms across his chest, his broad chin sticking out. His ruddy face dark.

Douglas dropped his voice, speaking slowly as if to a child or someone from another country. "You self-centered stupid kid. You think this is a scout prank, terrifying us this way. Letting us sit here half the night, your mother and I, while you—"

"Watch out, Dad. You might slip up and notice who you're talking to. You might actually see me, Bert, if you're not careful." He lifted his glass as if toasting. "The oddball, the goof-off."

Douglas unclenched his fists. Across the bare-floored room, his voice carrying, he said, "You don't know jack shit about it."

"How you've suffered?" Bert swung himself upright, cowboy with empty glass in hand. "Is that it? How much you miss Sis?"

"How much worse it gets later, being the surviving child."

"What would *you* know about it?" Bert demanded.

"Everything." Douglas's voice was flat.

Alison got up and slipped an arm around my waist, holding on, uncertain. We two women watching from the sidelines. Was this fight a reaction to the good news? A male way of not being knocked sideways by the near miss? By the relief?

The girl may've been thinking of her own wayward brother; how it might be if he showed up back in Savannah.

Douglas was looking not at his son but at the floor. "My dad never spoke his name again after he was shot down. Once I witnessed him almost kill a rancher who did. Every trace of my brother disappeared from the house. Every photo except the one of him in uniform by the aircraft was burned. Every scrap of his clothes, every pair of his shoes, was given to the foreman's family. The board games we'd played, the books we'd read together, the chemistry set, the tools, all the stuff we'd collected, went out with the trash. He killed my brother twice for me—"

Bert coughed. "Gosh, I—"

"I became the focus." Douglas walked across the room in two strides, standing inches from his son's face, his voice barely audible. "I couldn't take a piss without my dad monitoring it. I couldn't go for a walk without him going along. He gave away all the decent horses so I wouldn't break my neck. He took my car keys; he became my chauffeur. When I was off at Chicago, where he'd originally insisted I apply, he wouldn't speak to me. He didn't answer my letters. He refused to get on the phone if I called, but if I didn't he gave Jesse hell until she called me. I could hear him bellowing in the background."

"Gee, you must've . . ." Bert, stocky, seemed to shrink before his father.

"I was never as smart as Walter. My brother was the scholar, the brain. When I took the job at a school in upstate New York instead of getting one at Berkeley or Princeton, Dad turned into an old man. Nothing at all had come of his boys. One down, one who amounted to nothing."

"Hey, Dad—" Bert reached out an arm, but Douglas stepped away.

His voice rose, angry. "Do you think I wanted to do the same thing to you? Do you? Don't you see that the first thing on my mind, after the hurt of losing my girl, was you?" He choked up, turned his back again, and waited till he got control. "I was not going to do that to you. I was not going to fly down here and drag you bodily out of those goddamn swamp holes where you disappear for days at a time, leaving your mother and me with no idea whether you are still alive or not—not having the decency to let us know you've surfaced." Douglas threw his heavy highball glass across the still, white room, the sound sharp and shattering.

"Dad—" Bert cried out, afraid to move.

Douglas turned to me. "Why do you think I wanted all those babies? A houseful of kids? Because I used to pray every single night he'd knock Jesse up. I used to beg her to have a baby or get him to adopt a couple or even to raise one of the foreman's kids." He reached a hand up, seeming surprised to find his face wet.

"Sorry, Dad," Bert said lamely.

"What do you know about sorry?" Douglas turned on him. "What do you know about having your grief taken away? I had nothing left of my brother. They stripped the premises and burned his memory to ash. Now your mother is trying to do the same thing to your sister. I mention that I've talked to the preacher who's got her heart"—almost automatically, he touched his chest—"and your mother moves the length of the East Coast in order not to hear me. If I say *Bethany*, if I even say my girl's name, your mother starts in about something that's been dead since before the mind of man. Digging up some creature nobody would give a fuck about if it wasn't deader than history. I say my daughter's *name*—"

I felt my face flush as Alison hugged my waist.

Douglas sat down in a chair, his hands on his knees, not

bothering to wipe his cheeks. "—and my son does a swan dive into some swamp." He slammed his fist down on the coffee table. "Sorry? You're sorry?"

Bert looked from his dad to us. "Shit," he said, "I really messed it up."

It was hard to realize that Douglas had grieved so for his brother. The times he'd told the story he'd seemed to be talking only about Daddy Mayhall. Or why he himself had stayed on in graduate school. It must always be this way when you came into someone's life after a death. If Bert ended up with a new sweetheart, it wouldn't mean a lot to her that he'd once had a sister. They might name a child for the lost sibling, but it would be no part of the new girl's present. The missing person had already been cut from the picture.

I had grown up with just the opposite sort of absence. My mom, Mabel, going on and on and then on some more about all those babies she'd carried and lost—the entire population of an entire town, to hear her tell it. Focusing, my mom, on each lost chance. As if, had they lived—her children, all of them—they would have filled the White House and the marquees of movie houses and been the emcees of talk shows. Somebody. Her descendants would have been *somebody*. I used to long for just a smidge of visibility, of time, of attention.

How different my experience from Douglas's feeling of being in the spotlight, under the microscope. Amazing how two people could live together and fight together and love together and keep their deepest feelings secret from one another.

No wonder, I thought, that Jesse, generous Jesse, always told that story about the two boys, Walter with his thick red *Outline of History*, Douglas with his self-referential studies using tomcats and nut-nutty squirrels. Daddy's new wife had been giving her stepson back his brother.

While the young people gathered on each side of Douglas,

I went up past the wide stair landing into the blue-walled guest room. It only took one minute with a screwdriver to get what I wanted.

I came down with the mirror from inside the closet door. "As I recall," I said, holding the flimsy frame out in front of me, "we are the only species who can recognize itself."

"Where did you—" Douglas stopped short, seeing himself, hair going gray, face streaked, tie undone, eyes red. Or it might be that he saw instead a seven-year-old, solemn, in spectacles.

" 'And first, before we begin the history of life, let us tell something of the stage on which our drama is put—' " I quoted as best I could recall the lines from H. G. Wells which Jesse always recited.

The kids looked at Douglas and then at me.

"What's happening here?" Bert asked.

"Your dad," I said to my son, "and his brother were these supersmart kids. Jesse tells the story about the first time she ever stayed with them. You must have heard about it? About your dad, barely in second grade, carrying around this mirror, poking it at calves and cats and birds and squirrels, trying to determine who could see themselves." Brains with bony appendages, Jesse had called her stepsons. And I realized that it must be Douglas's influence that made ours so body-conscious. "Small wonder that you and your sister grew up to be such jocks," I observed.

"I'm not a jock." Bert looked aggrieved. "She was the jock, Sis."

"Come on," I said. "Diver? Runner?"

Bert kicked off his tennis shoes. He seemed relieved to have the topic changed. "You remember, Mom," he said, "how we were talking about the guy who went to the Pole? The Norwegian. I said it was to plant the flag ahead of those other guys?"

"I lost it on that topic, as I recall."

"You said he did it to get everything else out of his head?"

"I did."

"If you can believe it, I thought about that in Little Salt Springs. I was in this murky mess, because the rain had stirred things up even this far south. And I was focusing on this glistening dripstone in arm's reach when I felt something hit, and I remember thinking, Shit, back to the real world. I really did think that."

Alison had reddened her lips and brushed her ash-blond hair. "I thought they were never going to pick you up," she said, letting out a deep sigh, pressed up close to him.

He ran a hand along her bare, tanned leg. "You did it all by the book."

"Even robots have to be rescued," she said fondly. "They had to fly Dante II out by copter from the volcano."

"Stop it," he said, sounding happy.

Douglas lifted the thin mirror and waved it around. "The squirrels didn't see diddly," he told the kids. "I'm not sure they even saw the pile of nuts; they may have tripped over them. At that point I put the thing up and made my brother get his nose out of that book. We talked Jesse into toasting marshmallows. We thought she was just a new baby-sitter at that point, and Dad didn't let us eat that junk when he was home."

"How?" I asked him.

"What?"

"How did she toast them?"

Douglas propped the mirror against the stairs. He wiped his face, the tension gone from it. "Gas stove?"

Alison spoke up, looking glad things were okay. "My mom used to make those s'mores, you know, graham crackers with Hershey squares and marshmallows on top, in the oven. Decadent."

"Why don't I call Jesse?" I asked, and I did. Telling the story of Bert's scare over the phone, for him to hear and the rest of us to hear, too. Getting an audience for the story, making it part of the ongoing series of scary stories that every family has. Thinking, briefly, sadly, that it might have been just this way, the safe shivers up the spine, if our daughter's wreck had merely been a close call.

"How did you toast the marshmallows for Walter and Douglas?" I inquired.

She didn't even have to ask what I meant. "I rubbed a couple of matchsticks together, out back. Daddy Mayhall had this mesquite grill. Tasty, they were. As I recall, Walter ate two for every one Doug ate."

How many eons ago that was, I thought, before Jesse had Pettigrew the orange tom, before she talked to the goats and the Appaloosa. I was about to hang up when she asked, "You're on the island still?"

"Yes. Everyone is here—"

"Look in the cake tin."

"The *what?*" I had to laugh. A cake tin, at Sanibel? Shades of Mabel.

"On a shelf in the pantry. That's where I kept what I called the permanent food."

Sure enough, way high up on the tallest shelf of the deep pantry, behind a breadbox my mom would have been proud to own, was a Texas-special flowered cake tin. In which I found a package of marshmallows—which might need to be carbon-dated—and some chocolate chip cookies. Permanent food, as Jesse said. Preserved for posterity. I put the marshmallows on the cookies, making three per person, and toasted them in the oven until the sugary outsides were crisp and browned, the insides gooey, and the chocolate bits had melted and oozed. Not half bad.

Mouth full, Bert spoke to his dad. "Was he—your brother Walter, I guess I should say my uncle—always telling you what to do?"

Douglas looked as if he'd been handed a gift. He had a moment of difficulty finding words, then he said, "He was. Walter had all the answers. You know how it is, the older ones always think they know best." The men were on the white couch, legs stretched out in front of them: Douglas's longer, scholar legs; Bert's, in shorts, the muscled legs of the rodeo rider.

"Yeah," Bert agreed. "Bethany did that. She was all over me to stand up straight, why didn't I? Or get more exercise, or why didn't I run all over the county the way she did."

Walter. Bethany. How the men rolled the names of the dead off their tongues as if a ban had been lifted, a vow of silence rescinded.

"We get it from our parents, too," Douglas said, grinning as if they were just any two younger brothers, comparing notes. "They expect you to live up to the firstborn, but then at the same time, they want you to fill in the gaps the older one left."

"Tell me about it," Bert said, with feeling. *"Dad."*

"It's the nature of the beast. Mea as culpa as any. Just wait, your time will come."

Bert gazed over at Alison. "I guess I hope it does, one of these days."

When the phone rang, no one budged. What could get us now?

Finally, reluctantly, I headed for the kitchen, picking up on the fourth ring.

It was the heart doctor, Angleton. "I have a donor," he said, "if you're still set on watching. You'll need to get a flight first thing in the morning. And Nan"—he paused a minute—"I think you'd better tell that husband of yours to come along."

7

On the plane we traded news items. A load of migrant workers, I read aloud to Douglas from *The New York Times*, had overturned in New York State. They'd been to Maine to work the blueberry crops and then to Massachusetts to tend the cranberry crops, and were on their way back to Fort Myers, Florida, their home base. Had the truck not overturned, we might have passed it on the way going to the airport. The kicker was that they were bees, *migrant bees*. Twenty-four million honeybees returning from a hard month pollinating in New England. Imagine.

Douglas shared an item from *Science* magazine, concerning a doctor in Houston who was preparing amino acid derivatives for a new kind of therapy on brain tumors. The hooker was that the initial work had been done on urine collected in a Texas roadside park. Collected? Truck stop? Rest stop? We looked at one another, trying to comprehend science on the interstate.

We travelled well together. Airplane seats were soon awash in papers and magazines which had to be tucked in the pocket under the tray when it was time for the indifferent in-flight meal. It was a sort of time-out which was in its way comforting. We seldom complained about late flights, rescheduling, missed connections. Air travel was a holding pattern we welcomed.

Perhaps that was part of our nostalgia for Chicago. Chicago by definition required getting from here to there on public transportation. A complex coin-conscious trek in the days of class schedules and a new romance. We took the Loop, the Hyde Park train, trains up to the North Shore. We caught cabs, quick, cheap, always there. Lots of students had bikes, not jocks as at Douglas's university on the hill, but travellers, packs on, faces bundled, gloves lined, getting from underheated rooms to overheated classes, parking, locking up, taking off a wheel to guard against theft. How did you get here? a frequent, casual question. How're you getting back? another.

We left Florida at 6 a.m., changed in Atlanta, and if on schedule would be in a rental car at Houston Intercontinental by 9:10. The time change helping. I'd figured out that I wasn't doing quite as well as I thought when I found I'd studied the airline guide for ten minutes trying to make connections between Syracuse instead of Fort Myers and Houston. Where are you, Nan? How'd you get here? Where are you going?

We left the kids in the house, their faces appearing for a sleepy goodbye, sorry about last night, and then disappearing again. Jesse was right, the cottage on Sanibel would be a good base for Bert, later. Closer to all the underground caves in north Florida than Mead's Mill, for sure. And a place that had family ties and a feel of home for him, and yet wasn't our handed-down Victorian, full of his childhood, full of his sister.

Naturally, I was thinking over airline coffee, Angleton

and the heart center had had previous transplants that I'd not been invited to watch, legions, no doubt—hearts harvested daily, like grapefruit in the Texas Valley. But this time, as he'd explained, the donor was in the hospital, there wasn't such a rush. They were awaiting the verdict of brain-dead; awaiting the family's permission to shut off the support system. I tried not to think of them, that family, filling out those forms in that room. Tried not to think about the procedures done by the medical team before making that call. Rather, to think of someone waiting. Hoping.

"I think," Douglas said, breaking our high-altitude silence, "that as long as we're going down there—over there—" He had been disoriented leaving from Florida, too. "—that I'll go hear the Reverend Clayton preach. I assume that southern churches all still have prayer meetings on Wednesday. We've given ourselves two extra days."

"Good idea." I tried to make my voice neutral. Had it not occurred to him why it was that Angleton suggested I bring him along? It hadn't.

He leaned back his head and shut his eyes. "You drive when we get there, do you mind?"

"Okay," I said, not having known Douglas to voluntarily relinquish car keys before. Was it fatigue? Or, more likely, a visceral response to what we were heading to Houston to do.

"You take the feeder along Route 59," he instructed, as if he had a map in front of him, "then take University to Fannin. Remember, there's that short-cut through the Children's Hospital emergency ramp. We ought to have a break between the bumper-to-bumper work crowd and the lunch crowd." He rubbed the lines between his eyes.

"Thanks," I told him. Remembering, as perhaps he was, too, how still it had been the last time we were there, for the donor party, the streets strangely empty as if a parade had just passed.

He roused himself, reading aloud a piece on the Jupiter probe, in which a scientist was quoted as saying that the planet's upper atmosphere would smell like rotten eggs, and its gaudy poisonous clouds like rotten fish. "To whom?" he railed. "To life on Jupiter? To the Galileo satellite?"

"Anthropo-terrestrialism," I said, using a word he'd coined some years ago for such reporting.

"Will you come with me?" he asked, stuffing the magazine down by his seat.

He was talking about his preacher. Did he not suspect? Oh, Douglas, poor Douglas. "You mean to hear his service? Sure, if you want me to," I promised.

"Please," he said as the flight attendant served us our chicken with carrots and peas.

ᚨ   ⑥   ᚨ

Remind me why I'm letting you watch this?" Angleton had appeared at my elbow, already greened up.

As instructed, I'd left the car at the curb to be parked, getting a numbered stub. We were guided to the color-coded cardiac floor, where a receptionist had whisked Douglas away, while a nurse handed me a key to the observation rooms.

I'd worn slacks and walking shoes, and a linen jacket in case I needed a handy pocket.

"Because I don't know the people involved," I said.

"Because you saved a life for us." He offered me coffee and helped himself to a cup. He was a slender man with the hands of a piano player, strangely anonymous-looking, as if he kept himself well-concealed behind his work.

There were two plates of donuts by the huge stainless pot, and one of rich, good chocolatier's chocolate. I envisioned each surgeon going in to operate, tanked up on sugar, chocolate, and caffeine. What a high. Getting a fix like a runner doing the hundred-yard dash. Maybe that's what it took.

"We've got an emergency," he said. "We're already backed up. Your transplant should be in Theater Four. In about half an hour. Give or take."

"How does this one—look?" I wasn't sure how to ask my question. Or if I meant the fresh heart or the ailing patient. I was wondering if all the heart doctors had to be tall. So they could bend over the table? You didn't have an image of heart surgeons standing on stools, although of course the tables must lower and raise as required. Still, I'd seen other surgeons; they were all tall. The Tall Surgeons Club. Perhaps that was what kept women out of the field?

"Hard to tell," Angleton said. "Wait a second." He disappeared, then came back with a white lab coat with his name sewn on the pocket in script. "Here, this ought to fit." No doubt he kept such coats in all sizes for his visitors. I put my hands deep in the pockets and squared my shoulders. I became an insider. An immediate aura of entitlement replaced my sense of trespass.

I went across the color-marked hall and up wide stairs to the quartet of operating theaters. In films, the bystanders stood in more of an arena, a balcony, high above the procedure below. Or maybe they were med students watching their teacher. These resembled skylight domes and were much closer to the green-covered operating tables below than I'd anticipated. I took a little tour: two theaters on this side, two on the other. Nothing was happening in Four.

In One, a large man, buck naked, was lying on the table. Someone in light green was making marks on his torso in what looked to be a giant purple Magic Marker. Horizontal and vertical slashes on his abdomen. Some other intern shaved his chest hair and then his pubic hair, like a barber, while another taped the man's eyelids shut with adhesive tape. A nurse painted something which looked like iodine on his throat, put a clear plastic bib with a hole in it over the spot, and held it as someone else jabbed a needle into the neck for a catheter. Meanwhile, the anesthesiologist, who was setting up behind and below the man's head, suddenly glanced up, saw me, and angrily waved me away.

It must be I wasn't supposed to know that patients didn't come in covered. No doubt the gown the man had worn on the gurney had been tossed in the laundry already. I felt like a voyeur and left the room.

Maybe I was making a mistake and would feel like a Peeping Tom when the time came. But I had watched my babies come. Douglas had not understood at all when I stopped my labor with Bethany and requested that the mirror overhead be adjusted so that I could watch the birth. And that had been amazing, then, to see how that narrow opening in my pelvis, which had at first even had trouble stretching itself enough for sex, could become a yawning channel large enough for an infant's head to crown, and then close right up, as if a spring had been released.

It hadn't seemed to me as if my bones could have been that far apart. Later, at home, however, I'd measured the space between the pelvic bones with a ruler, and of course there was room. And then I understood cesareans, and what they never told you when you were pregnant, that in the old days when they had to choose between the mother and the child, they had to either crush the infant's head or tear the mother limb from limb.

In Theater Four, already, there was a woman on the table, her head pulled so far back it looked as if the neck would snap. An anesthesiologist was treating it as if it had no connection with the body on the table. The patient was being hooked up to the heart-lung machine, and everything was calm. Everyone looked attentive, at rest, a battalion before the siege.

A young man in green (tall, of course) looked up at me, smiled, I waved, he spoke in Angleton's ear, he looked up, nodded to me and to the man across from him who was assisting, and cut into the chest. I could see, down at the woman's knees, a bowl filled with what I assumed was a saline solution and, in it—a heart.

I, who had studied the outlines of what had once been sea-dwelling creatures billions of years ago, but which were now only the concretions that filled the spaces left when the animals dissolved and washed away, felt on unfamiliar ground. I'd only studied its footprints, in a sense, its hieroglyphics, and not the trilobite itself. There was no invasion in lifting a fossil from its surroundings. No sense of holding a living thing.

How different, how stunning, to watch a still-warm heart cut from a freshly opened chest.

The incision was smoking like dry ice. That must be some sort of cauterizing. I saw, when the new heart was handed up, that it, the donor's heart, was more fatty than the one it was replacing, with streaks of what looked like chicken fat on the outside, but that must be all right, not the same as larded muscle. I saw Angleton reach inside and remove what looked to be a clot or a string of something red, and then—quickly, surely—the damaged heart was lifted out and handed down to the foot of the table, where it was placed in another solution.

That would go to pathology, I supposed. Or else would be rushed to some laboratory. I'd asked before, in our daughter's case, and had learned that the recipient hearts, the defective hearts, were used to verify researchers' suspicions about disease and deterioration, to confirm their work on cows and pigs. Lab work always being a guess—if this, then that. They would look at the morphology of the new cells which the blood vessels in the occluded heart made to deal with plaque, say, see if they corresponded with the porcine or bovine samples. The tired worn-out hearts put to some use after all.

Now the donor's heart was lowered into the chest cavity and then lifted out again. Angleton took some shears and trimmed the valves down a bit, tried it again, snipped them a bit more, then fit it into place. The discarded scraps, which looked like pieces of calamari, were removed at once. Then the two interns watched as Angleton first squeezed the heart, then pricked it with needles to prevent embolisms. Everything ready, he began the painstaking stitching that secured it in place.

Then the woman was disconnected from the heart machine.

Everyone stood, motionless, silent, alert. The two doctors leaned, heads almost touching, over her, seeming not to breathe. There was a missed count, a visible tick of worry. And then the transplanted heart began to beat on its own.

I put my hand to my mouth to stifle any sound. It was incredible, to see it beating there, like a naked animal, like some sea snail out of its shell, left palpitating on the shore. And then, what I had not thought about, what seemed the most marvelous event, the woman's lungs began to flutter up and down. She was breathing. She was *alive*.

The machines were disconnected, and when they began to sew the chest closed over the new heart, I wept into my fists but did not take my eyes from the scene on the green table below.

I felt at last that I had shared what it must have felt like for the Reverend Calvin C. Clayton's contingent: the two dozen kin and parishioners waiting out the time, men resting their faces in their palms, women pressing scented lace-trimmed handkerchiefs to their eyes or stitching away at their piecework, all clustered together praying for that moment when the word came down: after two hours the new heart was trembling like a newborn.

I'd tried to tell Douglas why I needed to see this with my own eyes. "If you have lost someone you love," I'd said, "you are looking at it from that point of view, that bereavement. You can't look at it any other way." Just as he and I, Bethany Mayhall's parents, had sat together during the earlier transplant. Knowing only that the person who got her heart would have died the next day without it. That we had done a good deed. That the match was fine. That although the donor had to be larger than the recipient, our daughter had been an athletic girl, the person receiving it, slight.

But now I had seen it from the other point of view. Had felt the fear and then the relief when the harvested heart at last kicked in. Had felt the moment of astonishment when the still chest fluttered into breath. And had not for a moment wondered who had lost someone beloved.

I didn't stay for the scrub-up. My hands were damp. I needed to pee. I could use a cup of coffee. I took one last look and went down the stairs.

I found a bathroom that said STAFF, but I was still in my entitling white coat, and then, reluctantly, I gave the nurse the key from my jacket pocket. I didn't want to leave. I wanted to return every day. I wanted to see a hundred times that heart start beating, a hundred times the lungs lifting, expelling, sinking, lifting again. Life. I wanted to watch life.

It had not been the same when I'd seen the births of my children. Because the infant was alive all along. The baby came out, stretched, flexed its tiny hands and feet, and somehow went at once from breathing water to breathing air. And then they cleaned the eyes and placed it on your belly and you were proud and amazed at the two of you, and your breasts tugged, your milk grew eager to flow. But the start of life? No.

Not the clenching fat-streaked fist of heart that began to open and close, not the gray wings of the lungs beating the air. Not that single-minded struggle to give that one used body the promise of tomorrow.

☙   ⑥   ❧

When I saw Douglas in the waiting room reserved for the families of heart patients, I knew he'd gotten bad news. My husband looked as if he'd lost his next of kin. The preacher's wife, sitting by him, appeared just the same as I remembered, composed, kindly, and was stitching green petals around a red rosebud on a square of white linen.

"He's gone," Douglas said.

I couldn't help myself, my eyes filled. "I'm so sorry," I told his widow. All that work and time and anguish to fix the old man up. I felt as if I'd just watched the heart being put into the Reverend Clayton, had just been through the extraordinary effort of providing him with a new one, a healthy one, cutting it to size, waiting for the moment when it began to pump on its own, and then—all that for nothing. What unbearable cruelty.

The woman nipped off a bit of yarn with her teeth, then began, in a conversational tone, "Calvin C. started having what we thought was a stomach upset. He had had too many helpings of potato salad and sausage at the church supper—" She looked at Douglas.

He cleared his throat and picked up the account. "It wasn't until the middle of the night that they realized the nausea might be connected, and by then—" He choked, took a deep breath, his shoulders heaving. "It seems that sometimes the rejection is sudden, and masks itself as indigestion."

"I'm sorry," I said again, this time to Douglas.

"I didn't get to hear him preach," he said.

"He prayed for you every Sunday," the woman told him, laying a hand on his arm.

There wasn't much to say to either of them. I was sure if the older woman and I were alone, we would have found it easier to talk about death. That she would have had comforting words about how close to the rosebud the petals had to be stitched, or how to know when the length of embroidered linen was finished.

Douglas bent and tied his shoe. Trying to get control of his feelings. Straightening, he wiped his eyes. Then he stood and took my arm, his fingers closing around it above my elbow in a tight grip. "You would think," he said, lowering his voice, "that if this is a common occurrence, the nausea as a precursor to rejection, that the heart men would spell that out to the families. That at the first sign—God knows, we know that about heart attacks, that half the time they start out with gut pain."

"Douglas—" If he had seen a transplant, if he had seen one body being asked to support the life of another, seen the seconds of hesitation, or reluctance almost, before it kicked in and began its job all over a second time, he might have understood. That hearts could get tired of pumping, pared down, made to fit, sewn in place, not at home.

I became aware that other mourners stood around us, some respectful distance away. Women with bosoms buttoned up in good black dresses, lace handkerchiefs waving like white flags. Most of them in pearls. To one side, a group of men in their Sunday black suits, spit-shined shoes, white shirts, black ties, stood, feet apart, hands clasped behind their backs, heads bent slightly. When I smiled in their direction, they smiled back.

They looked almost as if they were a choir lining up, prepared to take their places, to sing about redemption in round full voices, proclaiming that Calvin C. had ascended where he belonged.

I wiped my eyes with the back of my hand, feeling too casual in my slacks and loafers, wishing, like the women and men to each side of us, I'd dressed properly, to show my regard.

"My dear." Mrs. Clayton rose and provided me a few plump pats on the back. "You mustn't grieve. Why, Calvin C. was given generous time to put his earthly affairs in order and get his soul ready. A nice gift for a man like mine who knew how to appreciate it. A person can't come to terms laid up with tubes in and doped out of reason." Her face recalled bad memories. "Your graciousness in sharing the remains of your child made a difference in the life of my husband, and of his church family as well."

"What about you?" I asked. "What will you do?" She seemed the type of woman who would get on with things. Do the spring housecleaning a few months late, or trade in the old Buick, or replant the azalea bushes by the front porch. I wanted to console her for her loss. Casting about in my mind, I decided I would send her Bethany's "star-padded" quilt; she was a woman who appreciated fine handwork. The colors went nicely with her stitched roses. And it would please me to think of it keeping her company.

"Myself?" she said, smoothing her black silk dress. "Myself?" she repeated, her tone suggesting that was not a matter lately on her mind. "I could use a bit of rest." She sighed deep in her ample chest, then held up her piecework. "My sisters want me to travel to the Holy Land, but I told them I've been working on this guest towel since Calvin C. walked into this hospital, and I intend to sit myself down and finish it now."

It wasn't clear to me, hearing this, whether she meant her

church sisters or her own female kin, but perhaps they all had equal value for her, perhaps they all had had their say.

"I could have addressed that with the preacher," Douglas said, reproaching himself. "We wrote about the problem of rejection. I should have thought—" He tightened his grip on my arm. It was clear he wanted to shoulder the responsibility for the failure of his daughter's heart to sustain his frail friend. As if he himself had offered it as a rope to the drowning and it had frayed. As if it had been in his hands.

"Douglas," I said, "you couldn't do—"

"We corresponded on that very topic—" he insisted. "His doctors should have—"

How could he not be thinking of the woman standing with us? Or the crowd of mourners?

"Don't take yourself to task, Mr. Mayhall," Mrs. Clayton said. "Remember, we're not the ones who make the decision about when a man's time is up."

He turned to her, looking distraught. Trying to hear her words and at the same time holding on to me as if he might fall if I moved away.

Mrs. Clayton motioned with a slight dip of her head, her glasses sliding down her nose, requiring a push, and then the crowds of people in their most respectful clothes gathered around us. Comforting this man who had given their pastor a fine piece of extra time on earth.

                      ✸   ⑥   ✸

I'd like to take the wheel," Douglas said when the parking attendant brought our car. And I knew this meant we were going to the municipal park where he'd first tapped his chest as a signal to the frail black preacher.

He kept silent through the shady neighborhood adjacent to the medical complex, the sort of area where young people were living in what were essentially their grandparents' old homes.

After a brief trip, he pulled the car to a stop under an ancient live oak. He turned the key but made no move to open the door. "I heard it from the nurse before she took me to the waiting room. While you were gone. And it was just like my girl had died all over again. Just like I'd got Jesse's call about the wreck and couldn't comprehend the news. I think she was still alive for me, Nan, in some way, as long as Calvin C. was living."

I nodded, my hands in my lap. Whatever he wanted to do—get out and walk around, sit here, go to the Reverend Clayton's church—was okay.

I'd read in the paper about a daughter killed in a car wreck who donated her heart (her family did) to her own father. Was that cannibalism? Was that incest? The papers had made so much of it. Front page, near life-size photos. The daddy having to go around being devastated by his daughter's death and grateful to her for dying at the same time. And not feel any anger at the one or guilt about the other. Knowing that not a person in the world was looking at him except to think that he was wearing his dead daughter's heart in place of his own.

And what was going to happen when *he* died? Would everyone have to grieve for her as well?

I couldn't help but think how Douglas was going to suffer during the preacher's funeral, at the idea that his girl was being buried all over again. I could picture the big satin-lined casket, the elderly man (in reality only fifty, Douglas's age) in his black suit and stiff high-collared white shirt, his red heart-stitched tie and red pocket handkerchief on view. Banks and banks of red long-stemmed roses fanning out on stands. And the specter of the young girl also gone.

(Did they take the transplant heart out and study that, too? Surely they must. I knew they examined the chicken-and-egg question of heart muscle in recipient hearts: Did the contractile proteins change because the heart failed? Or did the heart fail because the proteins changed? And that they studied drug responses, looking for markers which indicated a predisposition to heart failure. But what did they learn from the once-healthy rejected heart? I knew that Douglas would be unable to bear the idea of our daughter, twice dead, about to be dissected further.)

"Let's sit." He pointed to a cast-iron bench under the oak tree—the same bench where the preacher had sat months before.

I wondered if the balding man who'd trudged all the way up Mount Elbert, panting and heaving with the lungs of the young Sierra Club man's wife, was still breathing. For two.

We watched a few joggers going around the track that circled the park, a cinder track. Saw a few mothers in jeans with small children. Saw one couple holding hands. Donors and recipients, all, I thought, giving and receiving new parts for our bodies. False teeth, breast implants, prosthetic limbs, hair dye, nail polish, crowns on molars, chemotherapy. Where did you draw the line?

"Tell me about the transplant," Douglas said.

I didn't know where to begin, what to say. What a clamor, what a fight, all those resources, all the personnel. All to keep one person alive, one person whose heart might kick out next week. Did that make it in vain? What to say about the woman who'd had her chest wrenched open, her ribs propped apart with a metal vise, her heart cut from her chest, a machine breathing for her, and then, reprieve, the new heart filling with her blood, old lungs swelling with fresh air.

"It seemed a miracle," I said.

He buried his face in his hands. "You cried for him."

"I did."

He raised his head and looked at me with red-streaked eyes. "You cried for him, today. You didn't cry for her. YOU DIDN'T EVEN THINK OF BETHANY."

What could I tell him? He spoke the truth. I had watched the operation in order to stand in someone else's shoes. To see it from the other side. My grief was for that person, once so full of hope, lost. "Our daughter was already gone, Douglas. She died Thanksgiving day."

He took my hand and stared out at the cinder track.

I felt my stomach recalling that it was hungry. A good sign. Small ordinary signals of discomfort would be fine to receive at this time. A minor tooth throb, perhaps a blister on the heel, a bit of dust blown in the corner of my eye, a broken fingernail, a peeling sunburn. I said, "When I heard your voice in that cafe in Chicago, asking for a piece of apple pie, and the waitress explaining that it was strudel, the south Texas accent that all but had cowboy boots on it—"

"Cow-pony boots, Dad always said."

"I think I was eager to be with somebody from home. I guess I'd gone from being sick of home to being homesick for it."

"You said you were an only child, and I thought, 'Hey, maybe I could try that on for size.'"

I touched his sad-looking face. "Douglas, I'm not sorry I didn't make all those babies, but I'm sorry I didn't know what having more children meant to you." I stood and looked around the leafy park where we had watched a candlelight ceremony some four months before. "Let's drive to the ranch," I said. "The cows should be finishing their lunch about now."

a note about the author

Shelby Hearon was born in 1931 in Marion, Kentucky, lived for many years in Texas and New York, and now makes her home in Burlington, Vermont. She is the author of fourteen novels, including Life Estates, Hug Dancing, *and* Owning Jolene, *which won an American Academy of Arts and Letters Literature Award. She has received fellowships for fiction from the John Simon Guggenheim Foundation and the National Endowment for the Arts, an Ingram Merrill grant, and has twice won the Texas Institute of Letters fiction award. She served on the literature panels of both the Texas Commission on the Arts and the New York State Council on the Arts. She has taught in numerous writing programs, and is the mother of a grown daughter and son.*

a note on the type

This book was set in Granjon, a type named in compliment to
Robert Granjon, a type cutter and printer active in Antwerp,
Lyons, Rome, and Paris from 1523 to 1590. Granjon, the boldest
and most original designer of his time, was one of the first to
practice the trade of typefounder apart from that of printer.

Linotype Granjon was designed by George W. Jones, who
based his drawings on a face used by Claude Garamond
(ca. 1480–1561) in his beautiful French books. Granjon
more closely resembles Garamond's own type than do
any of the various modern faces that bear his name.

Composed by Creative Graphics,
Allentown, Pennsylvania
Printed and bound by Quebecor Printing,
Fairfield, Pennsylvania

Designed by Iris Weinstein